TORN TO PIECES

HARPER ASHLEY

CONTENTS

Prologue	1
Chapter 1	5
Chapter 2	9
Chapter 3	15
Chapter 4	19
Chapter 5	25
Chapter 6	31
Chapter 7	37
Chapter 8	43
Chapter 9	49
Chapter 10	55
Chapter 11	61
Chapter 12	67
Chapter 13	73
Chapter 14	79
Chapter 15	85
Chapter 16	91
Chapter 17	97
Chapter 18	103
Chapter 19	109
Chapter 20	115
Chapter 21	121
Chapter 22	127
Chapter 23	133
Chapter 24	139
Chapter 25	145
Chapter 26	151
Chapter 27	157
Chapter 28	163
Chapter 29	169
Chapter 30	175
Chapter 31	179
Epilogue	185

For everyone who told me I could do this. Without your words of encouragement and endless support, Torn to Pieces would not exist.

PROLOGUE

"Josephine honey, can you set the table?" my mom called from the kitchen.

She was in a rush to get dinner on the table for when dad arrived home from his business trip. Like every year before, she had a lot planned for us. Gingerbread houses, baking Christmas cookies to leave out for Santa, and of course, watching our fair share of cheesy Hallmark movies. My mom loved Christmas, which made my dad and I love it just as much. This was the one time a year we were always together. No matter how busy my dad's work schedule may be, he always managed to be home with us for the holidays.

My parents seemed to have that once in a lifetime kind of love. For as long as I could remember I dreamed of finding someone who would look at me the way he looked at her. Like she was the only person in the room, no matter how many others there may be.

I skipped into the kitchen and took a few plates from the cabinet.

"Smells amazing, mom."

"Thank you, sweetheart. I just want everything to be perfect. I have a feeling this Christmas is going to be more special than all the others." Her face glowed with delight.

She said that every year, and each year was better than the last.

I took the plates to the table and began spreading them out evenly on the plaid tablecloth. I heard the doorbell ring, and mom quickly brushed past me to answer it. I wasn't far behind her, eager to greet my dad after his time away from us. It wasn't my dad though, it was a police officer.

He removed the hat from his head and held it in front of him, a solemn expression marring his face.

A soul crushing scream filled my childhood home, and it took a few minutes for me to realize it was coming from my mother. She sank to her knees in front of the open door. The frigid winter air caressed my face when the officer's blue eyes met my own.

I didn't understand what was happening, or why my mom was now sobbing uncontrollably on the floor. The officer stepped around her and placed a comforting hand on her shoulder before taking a few steps towards me. I clenched my eyes shut and balled my hands into tiny fists.

I opened them again and tried to focus on my mom. Something wasn't right. Why couldn't my brain process what was going on?

Deep down I knew. Deep down I knew that my world was going to change. The officer placed his hand on my shoulder and I sucked in a sharp breath. My lips began to tremble. Suddenly our warm home was cold and empty.

"Josephine, come here." My mother called out to me with outstretched arms.

I crossed the room and fell into them.

"Your daddy was in an accident." She managed, holding on to me for dear life.

My vision blurred and tears welled in my eyes. A heavy weight pressed into my chest, and it was becoming harder and harder to breathe. I knew what she was telling me, but I still couldn't process it.

I swallowed the lump in my throat as my mother's cries sliced through me. How was I supposed to do this? I wanted to be strong for my mom, strong enough for the both of us. Pain seared through my heart as I tried to give my mother the comfort she so desperately needed. But when my eyes met hers, all bets were off. I crumbled under the weight as the realization set in.

As a little girl I waited for a Christmas miracle that never came. My dad never came home that night, and because of it, I wondered if we would ever be whole again.

CHAPTER ONE

I wanted to be happy for her.

There was a sparkle in her eye that I hadn't seen in years. Ever since that night we got the call that my dad had been killed in a car accident trying to get home to us in time for Christmas all those years ago.

I was ten and it broke me. My daddy was my hero, my favorite person in the entire world. One second we were huddled up on the sofa waiting for him to walk through the door, and the next, I was trying to peel my mother off of the floor as she sobbed. One of the officers took my hand and led me into the dining room to get me away from the heart-wrenching scene.

That was almost eight years ago, and up until a few days ago I didn't even know my mom was dating anyone. She met him online and they decided to keep things quiet until they were sure it was serious.

"When there are kids involved it's just a little more complicated, honey. We wanted to be sure about things before we got the families mixed into this." That's her excuse for hiding her relationship from me for almost a year.

. . .

Now here I am, being fitted for my maid of honor gown and getting ready to stand next to her as she marries a complete stranger. I've never even met him.

All I know is that he is relatively wealthy, has two kids, and lives in fucking Alabama.

I can't even put into words how pissed I am to be moving in the first place, right before my senior year, but to Alabama? What do you even do there?

This time tomorrow we'll be arriving at our new "home". Mom keeps saying this is the start of a beautiful new adventure and that I'm going to love it there. She describes it as a massive estate nestled in the bay, with nature and privacy surrounding it. While it sounds great, I have serious doubts that this is going to be as picture perfect as she thinks.

Not only am I getting an instant family, but starting at a brand-new school where I will know absolutely no one. This is supposed to be the best year of my life. I'm supposed to live it up with all my friends one last time before graduation.

Oh, how the tables can turn within a matter of days.

When we pass the welcome sign over the state border, I want to cry. Goodbye beautiful and sunny Florida, I will miss you so.

"Promise me you'll try to get along with Sean and his kids, please. It's important to me." my mom pleaded as we neared the driveway.

"Yeah, got it." I muttered in response.

I tried to recall everything I knew about the Miller family. Sean, who would soon be my new stepfather, was an attorney at a large private firm that specialized in medical malpractice suits. He has two children, a boy named Alec and girl named Allie. Their mother had apparently died from cancer a few years ago, and like my own mother, this had been the first relationship after the loss.

"I can't wait for you kids to meet, from what Sean says I think you and Allie are going to hit it off famously!"

All this excitement is overwhelming, but I try to muster up a semblance of a smile to appease her. Allie is in the grade below me. Although, there hasn't been much said to me about my soon to be stepbrother Alec.

"We're here!" Mom singsongs as we pull into a long, winding driveway that leads to an impressive white southern style mansion. There is a wraparound porch equipped with rocking chairs and hanging plants.

"Oh great, we've been transported onto the set of Steel Magnolias." I mutter under my breath, and mom shakes her head.

A man walks out of the large front door dressed in his Sunday best and flashing a bright, white smile. He's handsome. A girl, small in stature, comes to his side. I assume that this is the Allie I've heard so much about. Her dark brown hair hangs in perfectly placed curls, and her bangs are secured back with a color-coordinated clip to match the pale pink sundress.

I look down at my skinny jeans and two-sizes too big t-shirt and immediately feel grossly under dressed.

"Sean!" my mother beckons as she races towards her groom. "I can't believe this day is finally here!"

He scoops her up and twirls her around and I fight back the urge to gag. Allie is smiling and staring at the happy couple fondly.

I slowly make my way to the porch and awkwardly wave at the Millers, well two of the three. "Uh, hi. I'm Josephine, but just call me Jo."

We make quick introductions before Sean leads us into the house. It looks like something out of a Southern Living magazine, and if I wasn't so pissed off to be here, I'd be swooning that these are my new digs.

"Allie-Cat, can you show Jo to her room?" Sean asks, and his seemingly perfect daughter nods.

Such the dutiful daughter.

She takes my hand and pulls me towards the grand staircase that leads to the second floor. "Our rooms are on the second floor." She gestures back towards our parents, "They are too, but on the other side of the hall. We have plenty of privacy."

I follow as she leads me down a long hallway and points to a set of white doors. "That's my room, and yours is across the hall. You have your own bathroom, and a huge walk-in closet. You'll love it! We left it decorated pretty plainly, Dad wanted you to have creative freedom."

It's actually pretty hard to keep up this angsty and brooding thing I had going on with how great these people seem. "Thanks, Allie. Don't you have a brother?"

Allie gives me a sad smile, "Yeah, he probably won't be around too much. He basically just comes here to sleep. He isn't exactly the biggest fan of this new... arrangement."

"Arrangement? As in my mom and I?"

She nods.

"He's not so bad once he warms up to you, but that may take some time. The basement has turned into his cave."

"His cave?"

She laughs, "You'll understand when you meet him. He isn't the friendliest, not very good with people."

Great.

Not only have I been ripped from my life and thrown into the middle of nowhere, I'm going to be living with an asshole who already hates us.

CHAPTER TWO

After tossing my bags down on the floor in my new room, I don't even bother to begin unpacking. I need to get out of here, explore for a bit. There is a full-length mirror and I take in my appearance.

This won't do.

I empty one of the bags onto the floor and yank a black crop top from the pile. I pull down the bun from on top of my head and comb through my long, dirty-blonde locks.

Much better.

I grab my purse and head for the front door.

"I'm going to look around, Mom." I call out.

My mother's concerned face appears from around the corner. "Oh, honey. I thought we could have dinner together. All of us, to get to know one another."

I shake my head. "Mom, please? I just need some air."

She nods and gives me a small smile. "Okay, just don't be gone long. Be careful, you don't know your way around."

Sean comes around the corner trailing behind. "Have your license?" he asks.

"Yeah?"

He tosses a set of keys to me and I eye him quizzically. "I can take your car?"

"We're family, of course you can. We have one that no one is using right now. It's a Jeep, and it's parked around back."

I know he's trying to kiss my ass, but I'm not stupid enough to pass up some wheels.

"Thanks, Sean." and with that I turn on my heel and bolt for the door before anyone can change their mind.

The town is small, and all I've come across are a few gas stations and BBQ joints. A bright, blue neon sign catches my attention and I turn on the blinker.

Perfect.

A hole in the wall bar named *Shooter's*. If anyone's going to serve a minor around here, well this looks like a good place to start.

The air inside is smokey and the light thump of Lynyrd Skynyrd's *Simple Man* is filling the small space. I take a seat on one of the barstools and an old man with an impressive beard approaches me from behind the bar.

"What'll it be pretty lady?"

Score.

"Bud Light, bottle."

The key is confidence. He doesn't bat an eye and pops off the cap before sliding the beer in front of me.

"You passin' through? I'd remember seein' that face." His strong southern drawl lingers on his words.

Before I can answer, a hand comes on the small of my back and I tense.

"You're new around here." His voice is low.

I turn and come face-to-face with potentially the most attractive guy I've ever seen. His skin is covered in ink and his biceps are bulging out of the tight white shirt. He looks like a guy you'd see on the side of a bus modeling Calvin Klein briefs, and my stomach quickens.

"Mhm, I sure am." I lean towards the bar a bit and arch my back slightly. I'm no amateur. His eyebrow shoots up and the rest of the conversation takes place without words. His eyes rake over my body, and I return the favor.

He leans in so that his lips brush against my ear and whispers, "In my mind, we're going to have sex anyway, so you might as well be in the room."

I'm done for. I stand and allow him to lead me towards the bathroom, not giving a shit about the smirk on the bartender's face.

His grip on my wrist is strong, and that does nothing but turn me on even more.

I'm not usually into the whole stranger romp thing, but this guy is too yummy to pass up.

Once the door is shut behind us, he rushes me, hoisting me up onto the sink. His mouth is on my neck, peppering kisses down past my collarbone. I let out a moan, needing more. His large hands find their way under my shirt and grip my waist hard. They travel up my body until he cups my breasts, the callouses on his hands making this whole experience seem even dirtier.

I reach for my pants and fumble with the zipper, trying to remove anything and everything that is separating our bodies from getting what they want. My readiness seems to ignite something primal inside him, and he turns up the heat even more.

His hands are working furiously, exploring every inch of my body. I trace the ink peeking through on his shoulder, and nip at his skin with my teeth. Now the moan comes from him, and my inner Goddess screams.

"Where the fuck did you come from?" he mutters.

I giggle, "The Sunshine State."

"You're hot alright." he says, putting his mouth on mine. I part my lips and let his tongue thrust inside. The kiss isn't clean, it's nothing but a clash of tongue and teeth. Pure, lustful passion.

"Mmm. The taste of your lips makes me wonder what the rest of you tastes like."

His hand slips into my pants and one of his fingers slides down my crease. Another moan, and then he enters me. He knows what he's doing, that's evident from the start.

"You're so fucking tight." He growls, and I smirk.

"I know." I whisper into his ear.

A loud knock at the door brings me crashing back down to Earth.

"Fuck." He curses. "Occupied, Asshole."

"Out, now. Take it somewhere else. I got folks needin' to use the facilities." I recognize the gruff voice that belongs to the bartender.

My mystery man picks me up and slides my body down his, placing my feet firmly back on the ground. He looks over me and lets out an audible groan.

"This isn't over." He says. "We need to finish what we started."

I pull my phone out and look at the time. I need to get back before my mom sends out a search party.

"Another time." I say, trying to hide my inherent urge to jump his bones again.

"When? I don't like to wait."

"I can probably get back out later; I have to go play the dutiful daughter now." I try to lace my words with innocence, and I can see the lust flickering in his eyes.

"Meet me in the parking lot later, we can go to my place." He responds, and with that he's out the door... readjusting himself underneath the tight jeans.

I look in the foggy mirror and try to get the almost fucked look off my face. My lips are swollen and red, and my hair is wild. I do the best I can and head for the Jeep parked outside, ignoring the bartender shaking his head and laughing as I make my exit.

"You're back! I hoped you be back in time for dinner. Sean cooked a beautiful meal, honey." My mother is beside herself, the happiness literally making her glow.

"Yep, I'm back." I say, taking a seat at the massive dining room table. Mom was right, the food looks great.

There is a pile of pork chops in the center, and a few different sides placed strategically around them. He is really pulling out all the stops.

Allie shoots me a sweet smile and I return it. "How did your exploring go?"

I lie, "Pretty uneventful."

Just as I'm about to bite into the pork chop, I hear the door open and close.

"Alec, glad you could make it." Sean says flatly, frustration evident in his voice.

I turn to finally get a look at the infamous Alec and my blood runs cold. My fork hits the porcelain plate and my mouth is wide open.

"Josephine? Are you alright?" My mother asks, concern lacing her voice.

You have got to be fucking kidding me.

Standing in front of me looking equally freaked out is the obscenely hot guy from the bar.

CHAPTER THREE

"Josephine?" My mom asks again, and this time I snap back into reality.

"Yeah, mom. Sorry. I spaced out."

This can't be happening.

"This is my son, Alec." Sean introduces me, and I push out the thoughts of his muscles flexing against mine out of my mind.

"Hi, I'm Jo."

He says nothing, instead staring at me with what looks to be pure, unadulterated rage.

"Alec," his father says lowly, a clear warning in his voice.

"Yeah, I'm not doing this." He says and heads for the dark stairwell leading to the basement.

Sean rubs his palm against his face and apologizes for his son's behavior.

"Can I be excused?" I ask.

"Oh please, just stay and-" my mother attempts to persuade me into staying.

"I seem to have lost my appetite." I reply, and it's the truth. Now all I want to do is vomit.

When I'm back in my room I sink into the bed and bury my face in the pillows.

Idiot.

It'd be my luck that I almost screwed the asshole in a fucking bathroom. I groan loudly at the memory. What's worse is the throbbing in between my legs as I remember his hands on my body, touching me *there*.

I need to get him out of my mind, fast. A shower should do the trick.

I can't sleep. My stomach is growling, and now I regret bailing on dinner. I roll out of bed and try to make my way down the stairs as quietly as possible.

Thankfully there are leftovers in the fridge, but it takes a few minutes to figure out where the hell they keep the plates at around here. I am creeping around like a night stalker trying to keep quiet, but the microwave has other plans.

When the door pops shut the sound echoes through the empty kitchen, and I pause for a moment to make sure no one heard. Then comes the beeping from the buttons, and then the signal that it's done. I almost don't even want to open the door again because I know how loud it's going to be, but at this point I've come too far.

I can't help but get a kick out of the way I'm acting. I'm treating the warming up of pork chops like a hostage situation. I let out a tiny giggle and then go in search of a fork.

"The island. Last drawer on the right."

His voice causes me to nearly drop my plate.

"Jesus, you scared the shit out of me." I screech. He looks completely unfazed.

I pull open the drawer and grab a fork. "Thanks."

The look on Alec's face is hard to place. It's either burning lust or burning fury, and I'm not sure which of those terrifies me more.

"So, did you know who I was when you threw yourself on me at Shooter's?" His voice is thick with accusation.

"You're kidding right? You approached me. I had no clue who you were. We didn't exactly exchange pleasantries."

He scoffs, "So you just rip your clothes off for anyone who pays attention to you? I guess the apple doesn't fall far from the tree. I can see why dad is stuck in a bout of temporary insanity and thinking this whole marriage thing is a good idea."

Woah hold up. No one talks about my mom like that.

"Look here you insufferable prick, if you say one more thing about my mother I will-"

"You'll what? Tell your mommy that you tried to fuck me in a bathroom like a whore and now I'm being *mean* to you?" The smirk on his face makes me want to lunge.

"I'm sorry, but you seemed pretty into it at the time." I take a step towards him. My rage has me feeling a bit bolder than usual. I can see him grow the tiniest bit uncomfortable at my closeness. "In fact, I think you were *really* into it."

He steadies himself, "Nah, I was just horny and you seemed easy."

I don't buy it. Not for one second.

I take another step towards him until his back is pressed against the wall and I'm pressed against his front.

"Hmm, I don't think so. I think you saw something you liked, that you *wanted*." His hardness presses into me and I have to suppress a moan. I place my hand on his perfect, chiseled abs and let it slowly glide down his body until it rests on his bulge.

"Oh, looks like you still want it. Well, at least *this* part of you does." The flicker of shock that flashes in his eyes only makes this so much sweeter.

"Don't worry," I say while removing my hand from him and placing it between my legs. "My body is telling me the feeling is mutual."

That did it, he loses it. He takes both my wrists in one of his large hands and flips me around so that my ass is pressed into his groin. His ragged breath is on my neck which sends chills down my entire body.

He grows even harder behind me, pressing into me rhythmically.

"You are a very, *very* bad girl." he growls into my ear.

"You have no idea." Seeing this as my opportunity to show him who he's messing with, I free one of my hands from his grasp and drive my elbow into his stomach. Hard.

With the wind knocked out of him he fumbles several steps back before somewhat regaining his composure. "What the fuck?"

I smile sweetly and saunter over to my plate of food and scoop it up into my hands. "No, I will not tell my *mommy* that you are being mean to me, I can handle your arrogant ass all on my own."

I make the short trip across the room to the first stair. "And by the way, I don't make a habit of fucking random guys in bathrooms. Call it...What did you say earlier? A bout of temporary insanity? Clearly, that won't be happening again."

He says nothing, but instead watches me intently until I disappear around the corner once I'm up the stairs. Now that he can no longer see me, I let myself freak the fuck out.

Once behind the bedroom door, I turn the lock quickly and slide down until I'm seated on the floor. My heart is racing, and the throbbing between my legs is insatiable. I wanted to rattle him, size up the enemy. I wasn't expecting for it to be so hard to walk away. After the things he said, I wanted to inflict serious physical pain. I can't seem to wrap my head around wanting him to bend me over the kitchen counter.

This is going to be a lot harder than I thought.

CHAPTER FOUR

With the sun beaming in through the large bay window, it becomes nearly impossible to go back to sleep. I pull my phone from underneath my pillow, nine AM. I'm not a morning person, and if I want any hope in ever sleeping in again, I need some curtains ASAP.

I drag myself out of bed and into the bathroom. I can't decide if my dreams last night were sweet ones or nightmares considering they were filled with Alec Miller. I splash cool water on my face and try to wash away the intrusive thoughts whirling around in my mind.

I can't believe I almost had sex with him. I was so close to making such a huge mistake. Our parents are getting married in a few weeks, and then he will be my stepbrother. I'm pretty positive it's frowned upon to screw your stepbrother, no matter how delicious he looks.

I decide that getting out of the house and doing some shopping may help. Allie mentioned that they wanted me to have creative freedom when it came to my room, and decorating would surely be a suitable distraction.

I pull on some cut-off shorts, a basic white t-shirt, and gather my unruly hair into a bun on top of my head. A quick swipe of a makeup wipe gets rid of last night's eyeliner and mascara. I dab on a fresh coat of both and head for freedom.

"Mom?"

I don't want to dip out without letting her know, but I also have no interest in searching through this place to find her and accidentally run into Alec.

A sweet voice grabs my attention, "They're out tasting wedding cakes. They asked me to let you know." It's Allie.

I smile and nod.

"Oh, thanks. I think I'm going try and find a home decor store. I want to make my room a little more... me."

Her smile grows as she hops off the couch and runs to the kitchen. "Dad hoped you'd say that! He left his card." Allie holds out a gold credit card.

"Seriously?"

She nods and pushes the piece of plastic into my hand. "Of course! We want you to be comfortable here."

"Wow, okay. Uh, any suggestions on where I should go to find stuff?" I ask.

"There's a Home Goods about twenty minutes away, it's one of my favorite stores." Allie seems so genuine and kind, not liking her is impossible. She is the complete opposite of her brother.

"Do you want to come with me?"

Her eyes brighten immediately, "I'd love to! I'll get my shoes."

―――

Our parents were right, we did get along. Allie was funny and kind, and an extremely good listener. She didn't complain about my taste in music, and even seemed to like some of it.

"Who is this?" She'd asked when Brendon Urie's voice blared from the speakers. "I like them."

"Panic! at the Disco, one of my favorite bands."

When we get to the store, I grab a cart and begin to make my way up and down the aisles.

"So, what did you have in mind? Any specific colors?" Allie asked.

Good question.

"Not really, I like purple... and black."

She doesn't look too thrilled with my choices, and I imagine her room is filled to the brim with lots of pink. I shrug and she laughs.

She points to a comforter set that is various shades of purples and violets, "Ohh that one is pretty."

It is, I actually really like it. "Agreed, that's the winner."

We spend a good hour roaming through the store and throwing random decorations into the cart. I now have an array of art and prints to hang on the walls, fairy lights, lamps, and a few throw pillows.

Once everything is loaded into the Jeep, we begin the drive back home.

"Can I ask you something?" Allie says, and I nod.

"So, what was up with you and my brother at dinner? When you two made eye contact I swear it was like you already knew each other."

Fuck, I was hoping to avoid this.

"Uh, we actually did meet earlier that day... when I went out exploring. We kind of hit it off I guess you could say. Neither one of us had any clue who the other was, and when I realized he was Alec it caught me off guard. I think he felt the same way."

She raises an eyebrow, "Hit it off?"

Shit.

"Well, kind of. As soon as he realized who I was though, a switch flipped. I really don't know. I guess it's complicated." I have no clue how else to explain this to her.

She doesn't press, instead just smiles and leaves it alone. In this moment I decide I do really like Allie, and I feel like we really could become friends.

When we pull back into the driveway I see him leaning against one of the columns on the front porch.

"Speaking of the Devil." Allie says to me with a wink. I laugh, and she nudges me with her arm. "Alec, come help us unload the car."

I can't read his expression underneath the black sunglasses perched on his face, but he does slowly make his way over to the car where we stand.

"What is all this shit?" he asks, and I roll my eyes.

"For her room, so it's more home-y." Allie answers sweetly.

Alec peers in the trunk at the bags and groans. "Whatever. Just go inside, I got it." Allie pecs a quick kiss on her brother's cheek and bounds for the front door. She calls out for me to follow her, but I'm uncomfortable letting him carry everything on his own.

I reach in for a bag but he stops me, "I said I got it."

Deep breath, Jo.

"I heard you, I just wanted to help. Please reign in your crazy." I spit back at him, and the slightest pull of a smile tugs at the corner of his mouth. He is *enjoying* this.

Before he can interject again, I grab as many bags as I can carry and march towards the house, putting as much distance between us as physically possible.

He drops the bags he carried inside my door and then leaves without a word.

———

The music blaring from my headphones into my ears transports me into a different realm while I transform the dull, white room into something more. Annie Lennox's rendition of *I Put a Spell on You* has me moving and swaying to the beat. My taste in music is rather eclectic. My hips are leading me, and I raise my arms over my head allowing my body to feel the music, purely.

Feeling it a bit too much, my phone falls from my grasp causing it to disconnect from the headphones.

"Dammit." I mutter under my breath.

A sharp intake of breath causes me to jump.

"Dammit is right, I was enjoying the show."

I look up to see Alec leaning against my door frame, shirtless.

His entire torso is covered in black ink, and I fight the urge to run my fingers over each square inch.

"What the hell is wrong with you?" I scream.

He places his finger against his lips as if to silence me. "Quiet, sis."

Fucking asshole.

"I am not your fucking sister, get out." I say through gritted teeth.

His deep laugh rumbles all the way down the hall. How long was he standing there? *Whatever, it didn't matter.* My door will be locked from here on out, lesson learned.

I try to force the image of his ripped stomach out of my head. God that perfect V-cut led to all the right places. Why was he watching me? What the hell was happening?

I need to find a way to get him out of my system. I need something, or someone to scratch this itch. I grab the Jeep keys and my makeup bag, bolting for the door.

Shooter's here I come.

CHAPTER FIVE

The familiar, smokey atmosphere welcomes me, and I take a seat on one of the barstools.

"Welcome back, little lady."

I smile at the bartender and try to fight back the blush making its way to my cheeks. He is the only other person who knows what happened between Alec and me.

"Same as last time?" he asked.

I shake my head, "Something stronger this time, please. Whiskey."

He nods and places a glass in front of me and drops in a few ice cubes. "Straight?"

I nod again, and he obliges without another word.

I glance around the small bar and take note of the few people inside. I celebrate my eighteenth birthday in a few days, but no one here knows that just yet. For all they know I'm of age and ready to mingle.

A set of deep brown eyes meet mine and I can tell he's going to approach me.

"Well hello, I don't think I've seen you around here before." He extends a hand, "I'm Nate."

I take his hand and give my best flirty smile, "Jo. Nice to meet you."

"Can I buy your next drink?"

It always amuses me when a man asks permission to buy me a drink. I guess it's chivalrous or whatever, but when am I ever going to turn down free booze? The answer is never.

"Of course, whiskey. Straight."

He grins, "Are we celebrating or trying to forget something?"

"Maybe a little of both." I answer cryptically. I'm not going to sleep with this guy, but I will let him take my mind off Alec for a while.

"So, you live around here?" I ask.

He nods, "Yep, born and raised. You?"

I down what is left in my cup and Nate motions for the bartender to refill it. "Thanks, Gus."

So that's his name.

"I just moved here. You're actually only like the third person I've met, and the second that's been decent."

This earns a laugh from Nate. "So, you've been here what, a few days and have already had problems with some asshole? Point him out, I'll give him a stern talkin' to. Defending your honor has to earn me some brownie points, right?"

I roll my eyes playfully, "Ah, I took care of it. I'm pretty good at holding my own."

He looks me over, "Sweetie, I don't doubt that one bit. Wanna dance?"

I look down at my glass and throw the second one back. "Sure, why not?"

I let him lead me to the barely there dance floor. The upbeat country song playing over the speakers is not the type of music I would typically picture dancing to, but the whiskey is already taking away my inhibitions.

Nate seems to be a perfect gentleman. He's flirty, but is also careful to not cross any lines. His hand rests on the small of my back, not daring to travel any further South.

The front door opens and I see a familiar pair of moody green eyes staring back at me. I let out an audible groan into Nate's shoulder. "Well, looks like the asshole found me."

He turns and then eyes me incredulously. "Miller? That's the asshole?"

Of course they know each other. This is a small town, what was I expecting.

"Friend of yours?" I ask, and he shrugs.

"If you count growing up together since diapers friends, then yeah." Just great.

I try to lighten the mood, "Hm, I may need to rethink my dance partner choices if that's the company you keep." My tone is cheeky, and he smirks.

"I think you're fine right where you are."

Good, that makes two of us.

Nate twirls me and I try to keep my eyes focused anywhere but on Alec. In fact, I don't see him anywhere. Maybe he left when he realized he wouldn't get a rise out of me, and that I wasn't going to let him mess with my head.

"Nate, I see you found a new friend."

Dammit. Dammit. Dammit.

"Hey man, yeah. I did." They do that annoying bro handshake that turns into a hug and I want to sink into the ratty wooden floorboards.

"I'm getting another drink." I say flatly, but Nate offers his services instead leaving me alone with Alec.

"Really? Are you stalking me?" I ask him.

He laughs, "This is the only bar in town, get over yourself."

He's right, I'm being crazy. But he's the one *driving* me crazy.

"Whatever." I mutter just as Nate reappears holding a fresh glass of whiskey. I down it in one shot and hand the empty glass to Alec. "Thanks."

"Damn, where've you been my whole life," Nate's words make me blush, and he grabs my hands again leading me back into another dance. We leave Alec there, which feels like a tiny victory.

I let Nate have a few more dances before I pull away and head back towards the bar.

"Another?" I ask Gus, and he walks away to grab the bottle.

"Does Nate know you're seventeen?" Alec's low voice whispers in my ear and chills cover my body. I look at him and scowl.

"Would you stay out of it? We're dancing, nothing's even happened."

I realize now I have no clue how old Alec is. I know he's older, but he still lives at home, so he can't be *that* much older.

"I'm eighteen in a few days, asshole." As soon as Gus slides the glass towards me, I grab it and walk back to meet Nate.

"I'm pretty sure Alec is going to spill the beans shortly so you might as well hear it from me. I'm underage, turning eighteen on the twentieth."

He chokes a little, "S-seventeen?"

I roll my eyes, "Yep, seventeen. Sorry I didn't tell you, nothing happened though. I also really don't want to fuck up having a place to drink."

Nate still seems speechless, "You uh, you sure as hell don't look seventeen."

I know that, I've looked older pretty much ever since I hit puberty. My curves came earlier than all my friends, and I'd never really been lacking in the upper and lower regions.

"Yeah, I know. How old are you anyway?" I ask him.

"Nineteen." He smiles.

"Oh, so you're a minor too. I guess Gus is pretty lenient."

"And him?" I gesture to Alec.

"Just turned twenty a few weeks ago."

Interesting. I wonder why he's still living under his dad's roof.

"So, what's his story? Has he always been such a peach?"

I can tell my question makes Nate uncomfortable.

"Sorry, I know he's your friend. I'm just trying to figure out what his problem is. He's been a total dick to me since he figured out who I am."

"Who are you...?"

Oh shit, I'd left that out too.

"My mom is marrying his dad."

His mouth drops open. "Fuck, *you* are the step-sister?"

Every time someone acknowledges that simple fact it makes me feel dirty for what we almost did.

"That's me, or at least I will be in a few weeks."

Nate takes my hand and leads me out the door and into the parking lot. The sun is beginning to set, and a few more people are trickling into the bar.

"Look, I don't know how much you know about Alec but he's not a bad guy. He's just been through some shit in the last few years. His mom dying really fucked him up. Don't take it personal."

Don't take it personal?

"That's easier said than done, Nate."

He nods, "Yeah I know, just- try?"

I laugh, "Sure, I'll try. Hey, you wanna get out of here? I'm starving."

"Absolutely. How's pizza sound?" he asks.

"Pizza sounds great." Alec's voice surprises me, again. This is becoming a thing between us, and I'd had enough of it.

"You weren't invited, and for the love of God please announce yourself next time." My hands are on my hips, and he just laughs.

"Actually, Jo... I think it's time for you to go home." The smirk on his face infuriates me.

"Come on, Alec. Don't be a dick." Nate speaks up, but the look Alec shoots him turns my blood cold.

"Get in my car, Jo. Now." He barks.

"Excuse me, how about-"

"Get in my fucking car, or I'll call Mommy and let he know her little girl is at a bar." The look in his eyes screams that he's won this round.

Nate goes to say something, but Alec holds up his hand, "Stay out of it."

I stomp over to the black Lexus Alec had been pointing to and slam the door. I can see them get into a heated discussion, but eventually Nate throws his hands up in defeat and heads back inside.

As he walks towards the car, the corners of his mouth pull into the biggest shit-eating grin I've ever seen.

I am in so much trouble with this one.

CHAPTER SIX

"I wasn't ready to leave," I pout.

"You were about to leave with Nate." He responds quickly.

"Yeah, to get pizza. Then drink more. I'm not ready to go home."

"Order a pizza from the house and stop whining." I wasn't trying to whine, but damn he's infuriating. Why did he fucking care if I hung out with Nate?

"Whatever, now I'm going to be stuck with a brutal headache because you made me stop drinking. Though, I'm sure that amuses you." I cross my arms, completely aware that I am acting like a child.

"There's booze at the house, Jesus, just shut up." He growls, and my breath catches in my throat.

"Fine."

When we pull back up to the house Alec gets out of the car and walks towards the front door. "Go to the boat house."

I knew there was a smaller building built off the pier that rested right next to the water, but I hadn't been inside yet. Without responding I trek down the concrete pathway towards it. There are lounge chairs and small tables scattered around the deck, and when I try for the door it's locked.

Plopping down on one of the lounge chairs, I wait for him to return. It's quiet, save for the sound of various insects performing their closing numbers for the night. The only light remaining is the large beam reflecting off the water from the moon. It's so peaceful, and relaxing.

The sound of harsh footsteps against the wooden pier remind me that my company for the night is probably about to ruin the mood.

He saunters past me and pulls a single key from his back pocket, sliding it into the knob. It's dark inside, but Alec's fingers find the switch quickly. When the room illuminates, I realize this is essentially a party room. It's equipped with a flat screen TV, pool table, futon, and full bar.

"Holy shit, this is great."

A room like this is any teenagers dream come true. If I'd had something like this back home, the parties would've always been at my place.

"Sure." He mutters.

Mr. Personality, that's Alec Miller for you.

He gestures over to the bar, "Pick your poison, kid."

Kid? I'm going to end up punching him before the night is over.

"You didn't seem to think I was a kid when you were in between my legs." I mutter under my breath.

That got his attention.

"Not many seventeen-year-old girls are hanging out in bars batting their *come fuck me* eyes at strangers either." he spits back at me.

"Touché." He's got a point.

"What? You're agreeing with me?" He seems confused, which makes me giggle.

"I mean you're right. If you're used to picking up girls at a bar you'd probably assume they were of age, or at least close." I shrug, "Anyways, as for the poison. Got whiskey? I'd prefer not to swap up."

Still eyeing me incredulously, he hands me a glass and a bottle of Jack Daniels from the cabinet.

"Let's play a game." I say to him.

His eyebrow shoots up, and I can tell he's intrigued. "What kind of game?"

I roll my eyes, "What other option is there for two people getting to know one another? Never Have I Ever, of course."

He's chewing on the inside of his lip, so I know he's conflicted on whether to partake or not.

"Come on, you afraid of me finding out all your secrets?" I may not know him well, but from what I've seen so far, playing at his pride is the best way to get what I want.

I can tell by the look in his eyes I've won. "Trust me, I'm not worried about you at all. You first."

This is going to be fun.

"Alright, never have I ever done drugs." I decide to start out with a milder question and am not surprised when Alec brings the glass to his lips and takes a long sip.

He refills the glass and then turns his attention to me. "Never have I ever fucked a guy."

"Really, Alec?" I answer before downing what remains in my glass.

He smirks, "I knew you weren't a virgin. You sure as hell didn't act like one in that bathroom."

I wasn't a virgin. I'd lost it to my ex-boyfriend junior year after prom. It was probably the most predictable and basic experience on the planet. It was horrible, but to be honest I was just happy to get it over with. Since then I'd slept with one other guy pretty casually, Drake. He was my neighbor back in Florida.

My turn. "Never have I ever had a one-night stand." He drinks again but looks like he wants to call bullshit.

"I don't buy that." He says flatly.

"I really don't care what you buy. That day with you would've been the first, however it never happened." Something flashes in his eyes at the memory. I ignore it and pour the Jack in my glass.

"Never have I ever faked an orgasm." He surveys me intently

waiting on my reaction. When the glass touches my lips a wicked smile reaches his. My cheeks flush, and I am positive the pink tinge is giving away my embarrassment.

"Sounds like you haven't been with a man who knew what he was doing." That low, gravelly tone in his voice makes me stiffen.

"Next question," I say quickly, attempting to break the intense eye contact happening between us. "Never have I ever cheated in a relationship."

He doesn't drink, "I don't do relationships. My turn." He leans towards me until our faces are less than a foot apart. "Never have I ever been fucked on a pool table."

Jesus Christ. What is he doing? I can't help but to turn and look at the pool table to my right. I know the look on my face is giving away my shock. I don't drink, and the mischievous smirk on his face makes it hard to keep my breathing steady.

He inches even closer to me and speaks again, "Never have I ever wanted to be touched by someone in this room." That low, almost growl-like voice makes something stir deep within me, something primal.

"It-it's not your turn." I stammer.

"Answer the question."

He is making me weak. "No, because you're lying. You can only ask questions that you haven't done." I try to make myself sound confident, much more confident than I'm feeling on the inside. On the inside I am reeling. "I know you've wanted to touch me; in fact I think you still do. I think that's why you were watching me in my bedroom, and why you wouldn't let me leave with Nate."

The air around us seems to fill with static, crackling around our bodies signaling the thick tension. The shudder that ripples over his body makes my stomach quicken, and I instantly grow wet. I don't want to want him. I know it's wrong. I know he's an insufferable prick, and that if I give in now, he'll likely make me regret it every day after this.

His jaw tenses, flexing as he fights the carnal urges at war in his mind. "I don't want you."

His words should wound me, but it has the opposite effect. I can see him physically restraining himself from touching me. I let my hand lightly graze his forearm, "Are you sure about that?"

The moment our skin connects all bets are off. He rushes me, picking me up and my legs instinctively wrap around his waist. His fingers explore my body furiously, kneading and clawing at every inch. I let out a soft moan into his ear which does little more than ignite the flames within him even more intensely.

"I won't fuck you," I'm barely able to get the words out.

His teeth nip at my neck as he makes his way up to my ear. "That's fine, I'll just make you come."

I never knew it was possible to almost come by words alone, but Alec Miller seems to be tapping into a part of me I didn't even know existed. His fingers tear open the button holding my pants and in one swift motion he has them on the floor.

"Fuck." I moan.

When his rough, calloused fingers meet my entrance I open for him. It doesn't take him long to have me falling apart at the seams. "Do you like that?" he asks, and I nod, unable to speak. The orgasm builds rapidly, and when it releases, I collapse into him.

Effortlessly, he totes my limp body over to the futon and lies me down, surprising me when he sits down beside me. Neither of us speak, instead the sound of my labored breathing fills the room. My eyelids grow heavy.

I can blame what just happened on the alcohol... on the inevitable sexual tension that ensues when people our age have too much to drink and are left alone to our own devices. However, my last thought as I drift to sleep is that this felt like something *more*... and that terrified me.

CHAPTER SEVEN

When I wake up in my room, there are immediately a series of questions racing through my mind. How did I get here? Was that all a dream... a very realistic dream? No, it wasn't a dream. I can still feel his hands on my skin, and his breath against my neck. *Definitely* not a dream.

A light knock at my door brings me away from my thoughts. "Josephine, Honey?"

"Yeah, come in mom."

I still haven't gotten used to how happy she looks here. The lines around her eyes seem to show more now, but that's only because she's always smiling.

"Alec told us about the car, that the battery died on you. He went to jump it off this morning. It looks like you left a light on, so everything should be good to go now. Oh, and your room looks great! I love the purple."

He'd lied for me, and my mother seemed clueless about my escapades from the night before.

"Oh, okay, Whoops, I'll try to... remember to turn the lights off." I mutter.

A few more pleasantries are shared, and she leaves my room, no doubt heading out for another full day of wedding planning with Sean.

My head is swimming with a mixture of a hangover headache and thoughts about Alec. How did we go from hot to cold so quickly? I pick up my phone and slide my finger over to unlock it. The new message notification catches my eye.

Drake: I sure am missing our little rendezvous.

I can't help but smile. Drake had been one of my best friends, but one drunken night things took a turn in a different direction. We'd both been ridiculously single with no interest in that changing any time soon. We wanted that physical connection, but with no strings attached. People always say that it isn't possible to have that type of relationship, but we were living proof that it was.

Jo: Ditto. Visit soon?

The three dots to signify he was typing pop up almost immediately.

Drake: This weekend too short notice? It's lame as hell around here without you. Plus, I want to spend your birthday with you!

I would love for him to visit. I need an escape from whatever the hell is happening with Alec, and what better way than with one of my closest friends.

Jo: No, that would be great.

We text back and forth a few more times, catching up and ironing out our plans before saying our goodbyes. I know mom won't care about him coming here, she'd known his family for years.

I don't mean to think about it, in fact as soon as the thought rears its ugly head in my mind I try to shove it out. I hate that my excitement over seeing Drake is almost instantaneously overshadowed by my worry over what Alec will think. Will he be angry? Will he be jealous? More importantly, *why the fuck did I care?*

———

The weather outside was too perfect to pass up, and when Allie offered to spend the day with me on the beach it was an easy decision. The drive to the public access beach wasn't too far. I'd settled on a deep purple bikini and black sheer cover-up. Clearly, my color pallet didn't have too much variation.

Allie, on the other hand, is my polar opposite. She's dressed in a baby pink one piece with cut-outs above her ribs. A floppy straw hat ties it together seamlessly. She looks adorable, and a small part of me envies her innocent, yet mature appeal.

I couldn't look innocent if I tried, my curvy figure ensured that. My hazel, almond-shaped eyes were upturned- mimicking that stereotypical Disney princess look. When I was little, my Nana joked that I had eyes like Princess Jasmine from Aladdin, full of secrets and mischief. My lips were full and had a natural pout to them that seemed to drive guys crazy.

Allie's appeal was different though. While she didn't look like the girl on the cover of Playboy, she's beautiful, nonetheless. Her beauty is more of that CoverGirl beauty, natural and simplistic.

When we pull up to the beach, Allie explains this is where everyone hangs out on hot summer days, and that she wants to introduce me to her friends. I smile, trying to push away my antisocial tendencies. I want to be friends with her, and I want an ally here... even if that means playing nice with her friends so be it.

"This is Jo, my new step-sister." I receive hugs from the small group of girls who all regard me kindly. They introduce themselves as Kelly, Janie, and Steph.

"Nice to meet you." I say, playing the role of gracious guest.

We stretch out our towels and get comfortable on the sand, soaking up the rays and salty ocean air. When I left Florida one of the main things I was the most upset about was leaving the water. I'd been so relieved when Mom told me they lived a few miles from the beach, and that the house rested on the bay. *This* was my happy place.

"Hey there, stranger." A familiar voice beckons me, and I look up to see Nate standing over me holding a football.

"Nate, hey. You following me?" I tease, earning a smile.

"Guilty as charged, pretty lady. Hey Al." He turns and gives Allie a quick wave. "What are you guys up to this afternoon?"

Allie sits up on her towel, "The plan was to hang out here while the sun was out. Why?"

Nate crouches down near my towel like what he intends to tell us is deeply classified information. "If you tell Miller I told you I'll deny, deny, deny. There is a party tonight, at the old docks." He flashes me a wink.

"You know I can't go, Nate." Allie groans. "Alec would drag me home in a heartbeat."

That didn't surprise me in the least.

Nate shrugs and turns his attention back to me, "What about you, new girl? It's time you met everyone."

I should say no. I have no business being anywhere near Alec after what we let happen last night. "I don't know, I'm not really in the partying mood."

Nate scoffs, "Not taking no for an answer. You can ride with Alec, he's-"

I cut him off, "Not happening. I'd rather walk."

A smirk pulls at his lips, "Or I could pick you up?"

I consider his offer for a few seconds. "Fine, but when I want to leave you'll take me home. No questions asked."

Nate nods and hops up from where he was kneeling. "Bye, ladies. See you tonight, Jo."

When he's gone I turn to face the girls and they're all eyeing me with surprise. Kelly speaks up first, "You know Nate? Already?"

"Uh, yeah. I met him last night."

Then Steph pipes in, "We've lived here our whole lives and he's never even spoken to us. You've been here for a few days and are already partying with the in-crowd. Life is so unfair."

I roll my eyes at the girls. "They're a little older than you guys, plus you *are* friends with the ring-leader's baby sister. They view you as kids." I shrug, "No offense."

"Plus, when I met Nate I was drinking in Shooter's and he definitely thought I was older. I mean, I'm eighteen in two days so I guess the age-gap isn't too bad."

The look on their faces tells me that they aren't the type to underage drink in public, hell maybe not even at all.

Thankfully, Allie steers the conversation towards my birthday. "Have any birthday plans yet?"

"No, not really. One of my best friends is coming to visit though, Drake. I'm going to make sure your dad is cool with him crashing with us tonight after dinner."

She nods, and we go back to laying out in silence. Thank God, all this socializing is giving me a migraine. I take advantage of the quiet to plan out my game plan for the night.

I will not hook up with Alec. I will ignore him and focus my attention on Nate. I will make friends and avoid my asshole future stepbrother like the Bubonic Plague.

No matter how bad I want him, I will *not* give in to the deep yearning stirring within my body.

CHAPTER EIGHT

"What are you going to wear?" Allie asks as she sits at the foot of my bed.

I flip through the clothing hanging in my closet, "No clue, probably jeans and a tank." Her nose scrunches up in disapproval. "What? I like the casual vibe."

"I get that, but you are also going to be meeting some of your soon-to-be classmates tonight. Don't you want to make a good first impression?" Allie has a point.

"Uh, a skirt maybe?" I ask.

She hops up and pushes passed me, apparently deciding that she's better equipped to dress me. "This one," Allie holds up a black leather mini skirt. She runs her hands over the shirts, "With this top." It's an old band t-shirt that I had cropped. The shock on my face must've been apparent at her choice of attire for me.

"Hey, don't look so surprised. It may not be *my* style, but it'll look hot on you."

I slide the skirt over my hips and pull on the shirt. I survey the look in the mirror and am actually quite pleased. "Not bad, Allie. My black Doc Martens or checkered Vans?"

She places her finger and thumb on her chin as if she is thinking intently, "Doc Martens, go for the full-on bad ass look. They will eat it up."

We both burst into a fit of giggles. To say Allie was full of surprises was a gross understatement. "Yes ma'am. Whatever you say."

After applying a thin winged liner and some mascara I look over the finished product. "So?"

"You need lipstick, go with a dark color."

Who knew getting a stepsister also meant gaining a live-in stylist? I could get used to this.

Allie gives me her final stamp of approval and I head downstairs to give mom a heads up. "I'm going out, Mom. I may be late."

She turns the corner and her eyes open widely, "Oh, Honey. You look beautiful... but won't you get cold?"

I smirk, "Mom, its summer." I know she won't fight me on this, she never does. She may not like it, but she's always been a fan of self-expression.

Alec rounds the corner next and I swear he chokes on his drink when he sees me. "Where the hell are you going looking like that?"

"Party, same place you're going." I answer, doing my best to appear aloof.

"Fuck no you aren't." He spits, and my mom's eyes are darting back and forth between us trying to gauge where the animosity is coming from.

"Yep, I sure am."

He laughs, "How will you even know where to go?"

I know as soon as the words leave my mouth he's going to see red, and I can't deny the excitement it brings. "Nate should be here to pick me up any moment."

"Nate? Who is Nate?" My mother asks.

I grab my purse and an apple from the counter, "Alec's best friend. I saw him at the beach today. He wants to introduce me to my classmates."

"That's nice of him! Well, have fun." Clueless, she's absolutely clueless.

Alec still hasn't spoken. His face has turned a nice shade of ruby, and I take that as my cue for a hasty exit.

The ride with Nate is pleasant, but not noteworthy. His taste in music is decent, but he talks too much. I much prefer the company of those who could enjoy the tunes in silence. It's not necessary to fill the entire fifteen-minute ride with words.

"We're here, welcome to the docks." He gestures out towards the old rickety dock that jets out over the water. Around it is a large parking lot complete with a fire pit burning tall. There are dozens of people crowded around.

"Wow, good turnout." I mutter.

"It's always like this. Come on."

I follow Nate through the crowd trying to ignore the looks being thrown my way. It's a pretty even blend of guys looking like they want to eat me for dinner, and girls who look like they want to claw my eyes out. *Joy*.

He walks up to a small group of guys leaning against a metal gate. "This is Jo. She just moved here. She's a senior at Southside this year."

I wave my hand awkwardly at them and am thankful when huge smiles break out onto their faces. Nate goes down the line introducing me to the guys.

Connor is a tall, lanky boy with deep set brown eyes. His skin is a beautiful caramel color and his dark, almost black hair has a beautiful ethnic curl to it. His smile is infectious.

Kurt is short, stout, and seems to radiate an overall aura of positive energy. He greets me with a bear hug and it almost makes me forget that friendly shows of affection normally give me the creeps. I can't help but laugh each time he whips his head to the side trying to remove the strands of messy blonde hair from his eyes.

Finally, there is Nash, who I soon find out is Nate's younger brother. They look eerily similar, the only difference being Nate's skin is slowly catching up to being as inked as Alec's. Nash's is completely untouched. He's also a senior this year.

"V, Babe! Come here!" Connor calls out into the crowd beckoning a tiny redhead to come join us. She reminds me of a fairy, her stature so small, skin so pale, and her features so dainty. When she reaches his side he props an elbow atop her head. "This is Veronica, my girlfriend."

Their stark contrast should make for an odd-looking couple, but in all actuality they look perfect standing next to one another.

"Hi," she says with a voice that's equally as ethereal as her appearance. "I'm happy to have another girl around."

"You and me both, the only other girls I've met are in the grade below. I'm Jo." We both smile, and I have a feeling that a friendship will bloom between us with no problem.

Nate's voice breaks through, "Get this, guys. She's Alec's new step-sister."

The looks of shock on their faces makes me instantly awkward as hell. "Uh, Yeah. Not until the wedding though."

"Damn, Jo. Has he been driving you crazy? We knew he wouldn't take this whole thing very well." Kurt asks, clearly concerned.

I shrug, feigning indifference. *If only they knew how crazy he makes me, in more ways than one.*

"Where is the asshole anyways?" Nash asks his brother, and I hate that my attention snaps to Nate to await his response.

"Fuck if I know, probably in between some poor girls' legs."

Damn.

"Poor girl? I'm sure she's hardly complaining." Connor retorts with a deep laugh.

The nausea that hits me hard is unsettling. They couldn't possibly know what their words are doing to me. That hearing about him touching someone else so soon after me is awakening the vicious green monster inside me. Envy.

Brush it off, Jo.

"True, I heard he had some broad pinned against the bathroom wall at Shooter's the other day and Gus had to run them off." Kurt's words make the bile rising in my throat burn intensely.

Nash wraps an arm around my shoulder, "How does it feel to live with such a nympho?" I know he's only teasing, and I will myself with every fiber of my being to respond in a way that doesn't give me away.

"Honestly, I don't give a shit who, where, or when he fucks... as long as I don't have to listen to any moaning." My resolve sounded much more confident than I'd expected.

"Good to know, sis." Alec's voice fills my ears and chills break out over my entire body.

I whirl around and slam my fist into his arm, and of course he doesn't even flinch. "I told you to stop fucking sneaking up on me, tool. And stop calling me that, I am *not* your sister."

My unexpected show of aggression earns a horde of laughs and cheers from Alec's friends, and to my surprise a small look of approval from Alec himself.

He leans into me again, voice so low that only I can hear the words coming out of his lips. The same lips that were on mine not long ago. "Trust me, I know you aren't my sister. I think we established that last night."

Just as quickly as he appeared, he is gone again, arm draped around some blonde girl wearing practically nothing. The way his ass moves in those tight black jeans forces me to watch until he disappears into the crowd.

"Earth to Jo, do you want a drink?"

Shit. It's Nate. The way he's staring at me makes it clear he noticed me zoning out.

"Yes, several please." I respond to him.

I need to drink enough that I forget who Alec Miller is, and along with the deep urge I have to rip his clothes off.

Right here, *in front of everyone.*

CHAPTER NINE

"Alec, let's take this party back to your place." I hear Connor call out. The crowd had thinned, but the small group of people I'm with don't seem ready to give it up.

Alec leaned against a wooden picnic table, elbows holding up his tight body. "Eh, I don't know man. Pops has been a little weird ever since the free-loaders showed up."

Was he serious?

"Ex-*fucking*-cuse me?" I sneer through gritted teeth. That same blonde still clung to his side like a flea on a mutt's scruffy ass. She cuts her eyes at me and I want to claw them out.

He doesn't give me a response, instead just a smirk that makes me see red.

"Come on, Man. Party in the boat house." Kurt backs up Connor's request.

Bimbo Barbie pipes up next, "Yeah, Alec. I wanna see your place." The desperation dripping from her words makes me want to barf.

He looks up at her and flashes a devious grin, "Alright then, to my place."

I make my way to Nate's car and once we're inside he lets out a long sigh. "You can't let him get to you. He's like a piranha, you let him smell blood in the water he'll just keep attacking."

"Easier said than done, Nate. He called us freeloaders. Like I actually wanted to move here and live in his dad's house. Fuck that asshole."

We spend the rest of the drive-in silence, thank God.

When we pull up to the house, the guys file straight down to the boat house as if they've all been there a thousand times. Veronica hangs towards the back, seemingly waiting on me to catch up.

"Go ahead, Nate."

When he's out of ear shot, I turn to the Fae-like girl and she gives me a reassuring smile.

"Well, I'm a little-bit tipsy and a lot of a bit irritated. I promise I'm not always such a downer."

V shrugs, "I don't think you're a downer; Alec can be a handful. It must be tough. I can't even imagine moving my last year of high-school... *and* having to live with his moody ass."

I scoff, "Understatement of the year."

"You hold your own well, keep that up and he'll crack eventually." With a wink she's through the door, and I follow.

I enjoy hanging out with Alec's friends. Everyone laughs constantly, and every so often I catch the smallest smile tugging at his lips. Not that smug smirk that he offers up regularly... but a *real*, genuine smile.

"New girl," Connor says right before tossing me another beer. I catch it in my hands, earning a nod of approval. "So, you'll be at school with Nash and V this year."

"Yeah, looks like it."

I assume that most of them had graduated and were the same age as Nate and Alec.

Nash came to sit next to me on the futon, "It's a chill school, you'll like it."

Out of everything happening in my life currently, school was the one thing I wasn't worried about. It'd always been easy for me, the academics side of it anyway. Now the whole social scene is a different story.

"Maybe we'll have classes together." V's sweet voice addresses me.

"Yeah, I hope so. I'm not so good at making friends, it would be nice to see a few familiar faces throughout the day."

We sit around the room, the boys taking turns spilling outlandish tales about wild nights out and epic brawls. I mostly stay quiet, listening. I focus my attention on not looking at Alec, or Bimbo Barbie.

It's easy enough to do, until Kurt included him in a reenactment of a fight that had apparently taken place at Shooter's a few months before I'd arrived. As I watch him act like that... being playful... it's hard not to let my curiosities get out of control.

Seeing this version of Alec makes me want to solve the impossible puzzle that seems to surround him like Fort Knox. I want to know why he's so callous and cruel. I want to find out what had hardened him against the world around him, and why he's so quick to shut me out.

Kurt launches a playful punch in his direction and he dodges it effortlessly, instead throwing his friend over his shoulder like a sack of flour.

Right now, catching this small glimpse of the real Alec sparks a deep seeded determination within me. I need to know more.

The dull hammering of bad music is rattling inside my head and all I want to do is snatch the person's phone that's responsible for this horrid playlist and smash it. Alec stood against the wall by the bar while the blonde danced on him, pressing her perfectly round ass into his groin. He looked completely uninterested, which only made her try harder.

"Pathetic." I grumble, not intending to actually say the word out loud.

The futon dips under his weight as Nate takes a seat next to me, "You're right about that." His eyes are also taking in the scene. "Want to get some air?"

To be honest, some air sounded perfect. Instead of responding I simply rose to my feet and gesture for him to lead the way. His hand finds mine and pulls me out the door behind him.

Stepping out into the warm, summer air is incredible. I expect Nate to let go of my hand once we make it outside, but he doesn't. Instead, he leads me off of the deck surrounding the boat house and onto the long pier that extends over the water. There's a wooden bench at the end, and small lights perch on the edges lighting our way.

"It's amazing here." I say, and Nate nods in agreement.

"Yeah, whenever Alec first invited me over I flipped shit when I realized he got to live somewhere like this. Lucky son-of-a-bitch."

There's no animosity in his voice, it's more of a playful tone that coats his words.

"It makes this whole situation a little more bearable." I admit.

"Hey, it'll get better. Eventually, he will get bored with messing with you."

Will he? Do I want him to? To get bored with me?

"What's his story anyway? What's with the whole rebel without a cause bullshit?" I ask and take in the conflicted look on Nate's face. I know he wants to open up to me, but he also doesn't want to feel like he's betraying his best friend.

"He's just been through a lot, Jo."

"Okay, how about more direct questions. Why does he still live at home? His relationship with Sean seems really strained. He's twenty, why not move out?"

Nate takes a deep breath and looks towards the boat house to make sure no one has come outside.

"He did move out, right after graduation. Then his mom got worse, way worse. Sean kind of checked out. Alec moved back home to take care of Allie and his mom while Sean threw himself into work to avoid what was happening. Allie had just turned fourteen, so she was at a really tough age... pair that with a dying mom and absentee father? It was bound to be trouble. Alec came back and held down the fort until Sean got his shit together."

"Oh." That's all I can muster up the strength to say.

"Yeah, she got worse a lot faster than they were expecting. I think Alec will always blame Sean for it. He's convinced that his mom gave up because her husband couldn't stand to be around her, to see her in that weakened state. He thinks the broken heart sped up the process."

I blink back the tears threatening to give away just how much this story is affecting me. "That's horrible. I had no idea, Sean seems so-"

He interrupts me, "Perfect? The definition of a doting father? Yeah, he's tried his best to make up for his absence. Allie forgave him, but it just isn't that easy for Alec. He had to watch her deteriorate, be the man of the house. It was too much to put on him, I know that much."

I look out at the water, smooth like glass. I tune out Nate's voice as he continues.

Alec isn't a monster, he's broken. He's angry at the world for taking away his mother. He's angry that the person who should've been his rock- his role model... acted like a coward.

He's also angry that his father is moving on and marrying someone new... and I'm guilty by association.

CHAPTER TEN

I stayed on the bench with Nate for a little longer, until the door opens and the crew begins to file out. Kurt's eyes meet ours and he smirks, offering a thumbs up. I roll my eyes and Nate laughs. I think Kurt is my favorite of the bunch.

When Alec appears through the doorway his icy gaze meets mine and damn near freezes me solid. That's until his little tart runs up behind him, wrapping her arms around his waist. Yeah, now my whole body's on fire.

Why. The. Fuck. Was. I. Jealous?

"Nate, take Cass home."

Blonde Bimbo has a name, and she's not happy. "What? Alec, I thought-"

He waves her off, "You thought wrong."

Nate still hasn't moved. I think he's equally as confused at the events unfolding around us.

"Nate?" Alec barked, and this time he rose.

"I heard you, man. Uh, Jo... I guess I'll see you later?"

I nod and give him a short one-arm hug before he leaves taking a very disgruntled Cass with him.

My eyebrows are raised so high that it's entirely possible they've become one with my hairline. "What the hell was that about?" I ask, and he says nothing. Instead slamming the door to the boat house and locking it.

"Alec?" I try again, and again but am ignored. His long legs take quick strides up towards the house, and I do exactly what my brain is screaming at me not to do.

I follow him.

When I come face to face with the dark staircase that leads to the unknown, I take a few deep breaths before making my descent.

Okay. You can do this.
He's just a guy, and he's in pain.
He needs a friend.
I can be his friend.

My feet creak against the wooden stairs. "Alec? It's Jo..."

His deep voice cuts through me. "I know who it is, no one else is stupid enough to come in my fucking room."

Stay calm, don't get angry.

"Are- are you alright? You seemed upset outside."

Laughing, he's laughing. It isn't a pleasant laughter either, it's harsh. He's laughing at me.

"Seriously? Do you think you can just walk down here and I'll crack wide open for you? Tell you all my deepest, darkest secrets? Tell you about what keeps me up at night?"

No. I didn't think it would be that easy.

I take a step towards him and he stills. "I just wanted to make sure you're okay. I don't know what you're going through, and I won't pretend to. I also won't pretend that I don't see you hurting. You don't have to like me, hell I don't give a shit either way."

Lie number one.

"We do live in the same house though, and we're going to have to see a good bit of each other. I don't want to be enemies, Alec. I know some shit has gone down between us, and I don't know how to feel about any of it. I do know that I don't want to walk on eggshells in my own home though. Can we at least try to be friends?"

Lie number two. I don't know what I want from Alec Miller, but *just friends* isn't it.

"Friends?" he asks, clearly not convinced.

"Would that be so bad?"

He takes a few steps towards me, and this time I'm the one who can't move.

"I don't do well with friends I want to fuck, even if it is *just* a hate fuck."

I cough, choking on the words he just so nonchalantly spoke.

"Yeah, that's right. I don't want to be your friend. I want you and your mother out of my house and away from my family. I want you to stop playing footsie with my best friend before I have to beat the shit out of him, and I want you to stop looking at me like some puppy you want to adopt from the damn shelter. I'm not your project. I'm not *yours* to fix. Now if between now and you getting the hell out of here you want a good, hard fuck- well you know where to find me. If not, then just stay the hell away from me."

My skin heats up, and a lump forms in the base of my throat. Tears prick at my eyes, but I fight them back. I fight them with everything I have inside me.

"I don't believe you. I don't believe that you are as heartless as you pretend to be. If you want to act like my mom and I are horrible people, fine- whatever. I can't force you to see us for who we really are. I can however, refuse to just lay down and give up, and I won't. I'm not a quitter. You are battling some serious demons, Alec Miller. Whether you like it or not, I'm here for the long haul."

Silence fills the room save for the sound of my ragged breaths and pounding heart. He stares at me with wild eyes, and I can't tell if he wants to kiss me or kill me. Probably a little bit of both.

"I don't know what all happened with your mom, but I do know that you stepped up and were there for her and Allie. I also know that means there is more to you than this surly dickwad facade you put on for everyone around you. I see right through you, Alec."

Jesus Christ, I wish he'd say something.

"If you think you can fix me...well, you're going to end up very disappointed at the end of all this." His voice is low, tortured.

I shrug, and what I say next earns the tiniest trace of a smile from his hard-lined lips. "I'm used to disappointment, maybe for once I'll be pleasantly surprised."

I decide to press my luck, "So, friends?"

He scoffs, "Woah there, Sally. How about for starters I try not to be such a... what did you call me? A dickwad?"

I laugh awkwardly, "Okay, that sounds like a good place to start. And... uhm maybe don't talk about fucking me?"

He closes the space between us. "Eh, I don't think so. I like watching you squirm."

"That's pretty dickwad-ish, Alec." I deadpan.

"Baby steps, Jo. Baby steps." He palms my cheek with his large hand. "Don't act like you don't want it too."

There goes my heart again, pounding in my chest.

"That'll have to wait, though. I got to take care of something." He drops his hand and crosses the room, grabbing his keys from the dresser.

"Wh-what? You're leaving?" I hate the desperation in my voice. I sound like Cass.

"Yeah."

That's it? *Yeah?*

"Uh, where are you going?" I ask, knowing good and damn well he isn't going to tell me.

That mischievous smirk graces his lips. "None of your business, Jo. Run along."

"You lasted all of thirty seconds without being a dickwad. Congratulations." I spit out as I make my way towards the stairs. His hand clasps around my wrist and he pulls me back towards him.

"Shooter's, with Nate. We're meeting for pool. Try not to miss me too much."

Satisfied I nod, "Don't worry, I won't."

Lie number three.

I'm going to miss him. I'm going to miss the electricity ripping through my body every time he's near me.

He lets go of my wrist and tilts his head towards the stairs, signaling for me to take my leave. And I do, I walk up them without another word.

When I reach the safety of my own room, I let myself come apart, reeling over my latest interaction with him.

Collapsing into the bed I can't seem to wipe the massive shit-eating grin off my face. Alec Miller was *trying* to be nice to me, and that alone is enough to make me feel like I'd accomplished something miraculous.

CHAPTER ELEVEN

Today is my birthday, which also means Drake will be arriving any moment to spend the weekend with me. Sean has no problem with it, and Allie helps me prepare the guest room with fresh towels.

"So, is this your boyfriend?" She asks, that spark of curiosity alive in her eyes.

"Hell no, we've been really good friends for as long as I can remember."

She doesn't look convinced, "But he likes you?"

I stifle a laugh, "Not like that. We've hooked up before, but that was just a combination of boredom and loneliness. We keep things clean and simple."

Allie lets out a hmmm but drops it. I understand that people don't think it's possible for a guy and a girl to have the type of relationship we do, but it works for us. Plus, we'd agreed when I moved that there would be no more casual sex... only friendship.

"What's this about?" Alec asks from the doorway, gesturing towards the folded towels at the foot of the bed.

"Jo's *not* boyfriend is coming to stay with us for the weekend, for her birthday."

I blush immediately at her words and regard him carefully... trying to gauge his reaction. His gaze meets mine and I can see the muscles around his jaw tensing. He said nothing, instead turning away and retreating down the hallway.

A few hours later a honk from outside alerts me that Drake has arrived, and I run outside to greet him. I jump into his arms and he swings me around in a circle before planting my feet firmly back on solid ground. "Jo! Nice digs, can I move in?"

I laugh and bury him in a massive bear hug. "I missed you!" I turn to look at my home, "It's pretty great, huh?"

Allie appears on the patio and I introduce her to Drake, and then lead him inside to meet Sean. My mother is thrilled to see him and spends the next several minutes asking how his parents are holding up with the new and *less awesome* neighbors.

As predicted Alec remains in his dungeon, refusing to play nice and introduce himself. "Sean's son lives downstairs, he's not exactly a people person. Don't take it personal if he doesn't speak to you." I find myself trying to explain and make excuses for his shit behavior.

"No worries, I'm here for you JoJo. How's about a tour?" Drake's face is permanently stamped with a mega-watt smile that makes my heart burst. I had made friends since arriving here, of course... but there's nothing like the company of one of my truest and oldest friends. As we make our way through the house he oohs and ahhs over the grandness of it all.

"This is seriously incredible. How the hell did you get so lucky and wind up living with Daddy Warbucks?" I know he's kidding, but Alec's comment about us being freeloaders immediately flashes in my mind.

"Hey, uh... maybe tone down the comments? Alec is pretty sensitive about shit like that. I think he's already convinced himself mom is a gold-digger up to no good."

A mixture of shock and anger registers on his face, "What the fuck? Your mom is a saint."

"I know, but he doesn't know her yet. He will though, it'll just take time. Try not to make any more *holy shit your new family is so rich* comments please."

"Noted, sorry JoJo."

That name, God I hate that nickname. Drake knows that though, and it explains the boyish grin on his face when I narrow my eyes at him.

"Wanna watch a movie?" I ask, directing him into the den.

"Only if it's Indiana Jones." He responds.

"Well, duh. What'd you expect?"

This has been a tradition since we were in middle school. The day of my birthday is always spent binge watching the Indiana Jones movies with popcorn and ice cream. Even though we'd graduated into more illicit recreational activities, this is one tradition we always stuck to.

"Jock, start the engine!" Drake called out as he plopped onto a large white sofa.

Laughter filled the room and I allowed myself to relax completely. This is exactly what I needed.

"Dinner!"

My mother's voice trailed up the stairs as she summoned us to the table. She'd made my favorite, breakfast for dinner. My plate was covered in scrambled eggs with cheese, bacon, and two waffles.

"Thanks mom, it looks amazing."

Drake nods enthusiastically, "Yes ma'am, this is perfect."

Everyone is here at the table, everyone *except* Alec. I keep watching the door, waiting on him to bust in late. Late is better than not showing at all.

When my mom brings out the cookie cake decorated with my name in chocolate icing I hesitate before blowing out my candles. "Where's Alec?" I direct the question at Sean, but he shrugs.

His face loses the bright smile that'd been there only seconds before. "I don't know, Josephine. He should've been here."

"Oh, its fine, I was just curious." I don't know why I expected him to come. I tried not to be disappointed, but it's impossible. He hadn't made me any promises, and he sure as hell didn't owe me anything. What hurt is that he didn't *want* to be here.

I blow out the candles and laugh when Drake wipes a bit of the icing on my nose.

Eighteen. I'm finally an adult. Even though I'd acted a good bit older than I really was for a while now, it's official.

I knew Drake was tired from the drive today, and to be honest I just wanted to spend my night at home. We settled back into the den on one of the sofas and put in The Kingdom of the Crystal Skull, and it didn't take long for us both to doze off.

I have no clue how long I'd asleep, but when I wake up from being gently shaken, the DVD menu is repeating on a loop.

"Get up."

Dammit, Alec.

"What? What are you doing?" I ask him, my voice sounding obviously groggy.

"Come with me."

I'm not going anywhere with him. "No, let me go back to sleep."

"Hurry, it's important." His words are slurred, and I know he'd been out drinking.

I sit up from the sofa and stare daggers at him, "Alec, you're drunk. And you missed my birthday dinner. In fact, your sorry ass didn't even tell me happy birthday. Screw off."

His hands are on my waist, hoisting me into his arms as if it takes not a bit of effort. "Alec, fuck. What is-"

"*Shhhh*... You're going to wake up your boyfriend."

The way he lingers on the word boyfriend sends a chill down my spine. "He isn't my boyfriend, you know that."

He doesn't put me down, instead he cradles me in his arms and walks out of the room. I want to keep asking questions, but something tells me to keep my mouth shut. He walks me down the first flight of stairs, and then down the next into the basement.

"Are you mad at me?" He asks before setting me down on his bed.

Fuck. I'm on his bed.

"Yes." I answer honestly.

He bites his lip, "Why?"

Why am I mad? I'm mad because my dumb ass set expectations for someone who very plainly told me not to ever have any. "You missed my birthday."

"No, I didn't." He held up his phone and showed me the time.

11:56

"Happy Birthday, Jo."

Such a small gesture in the grand scheme of things, but nonetheless it meant the world to me. Alec is an inherently selfish human being, or at least that's what he wants everyone to think, but he'd thought of me. He'd wanted to give me this one small thing, to prove that he was *trying*.

CHAPTER TWELVE

You could've heard a pin drop in his room. I'm speechless, and he's clearly waiting on me to break the silence. My heart might explode, and it's taking every ounce of self-control not to launch myself at him. I want to kiss him. I want to feel the way he'd made me feel at the bar and in the boat house. I want him to make me feel alive.

"Th-thank you. I don't know what to say."

"Then just don't say anything. I'm better with action than words anyways." He takes my face in his hands and when his lips press against mine, I melt. I melt into him not giving a single fuck how wrong it is, not caring that the only reason he's giving me this level of intimacy is because he's drunk.

This kiss is different than the ones before. This one was softer, but at the same time more intense. His grip isn't strong, but gentle... like he doesn't want to hurt me. I crave more. I *need* more.

Alec pulls me into his lap without breaking contact. The tenderness in his touch this time is intoxicating.

When he pauses for a moment I try to pull him back into me, desperate for this to not end. His lips turn up into a smile. *He's happy*.

A noise from upstairs breaks us apart and both our bodies go rigid. Someone is rustling through the refrigerator, and I let out the tiniest giggle. The risk... the fact that we can be caught at any moment is exhilarating. He silences me with another kiss.

"You should go, before someone finds us like this. I don't think this would be easy to explain."

I know he's right, but the thought of walking up those stairs and away from him right now seems impossible.

When I don't move immediately, he lets out a deep breath.

"Alec, what does this mean?" I ask, my voice barely audible.

"I don't know." He answers honestly.

For tonight that's the best I can hope for.

———

When I join Drake at the table for breakfast the next morning I can't help but watch the stairs. It's early, and Alec is probably not going to be awake any time soon. Still, my stomach is doing flips at the thought that he may waltz into the room at any moment.

"So, the beach?" Drake asks with a mouth full of cereal.

"Yes, you neanderthal."

I invited Allie to join us too, and she'd agreed. After placing my bowl in the sink I start up towards my room, "Going to change."

Drake said something that sounded like "Okay," but it was hard to tell. As disgusting as his eating habits may be, I still love the dumbass.

I decide on a basic black bikini and slide on a pair of high waisted blue jean shorts over the top. I tie my hair in a loose braid and apply a thin layer of make-up to my face.

Not too shabby. I think to myself, taking in my appearance in the full-length mirror.

I bound down the stairs and run smack-dab into Nate. "Shit, sorry. I totally wasn't paying attention."

He flashes his signature smile and shrugs, "Hey, I'm not complaining. Why are you in such a hurry?"

I take two steps back, putting a safe distance between us. "One of my friends is in town from Florida. We're going to the beach."

"Oh, you weren't going to introduce me to her?" He feigns hurt.

I giggle, "*His* name is Drake, but I'd be happy to introduce you."

Nate scrunches his nose up, clearly disappointed that I'm not having a girly slumber party. As if on cue Drake enters the room and one bro-shake later he and Nate are chatting it up about some obscure sporting event that I could care less about.

"Nate, what are you up to today?" I ask him.

"About to wake up Prince Charming down there," he gestures towards the basement. "He got pretty lit last night."

Yeah, I know.

"Oh, really? Did you guys go to a party?" I try to make my questions seem like normal conversation and not give away that I just want to know what Alec had been up to.

"Yeah, at Cass's place. Shit was crazy."

My stomach drops.

"The girl that was over here, right? That you took home?"

Nate nods and kicks off his sneakers by the door. "The very same."

He isn't giving up much information, and I don't know how to press for more without being obvious.

"It didn't seem like her and Alec left on good terms that day," I say with a laugh. "I guess I'm surprised he wanted to hang out with her."

Nate seems oblivious, but Allie's eyebrow raises. *Smooth, real smooth Jo.*

"Nah, everyone knows Alec is a moody bastard. You have to take his tantrums with a grain of salt. He seemed to have forgiven her last night, if you know what I mean." He gives me a wink and I want to throw up.

"Since when do you gossip like a girl, Nate?" Alec appears out of nowhere.

"Morning, Sunshine. Just swapping war stories from last night. How's your head?" Nate responds with a laugh.

Alec's eyes meet mine and I can't read him at all. Did he hear me asking questions? What had he done with Cass? Had he *been* with her before coming to me? I need to get out of here before my mind wanders wild with *what-ifs*.

"Anyways, we need to get going. Don't want to miss the sun." I spit out and pick up my bag from the table.

Alec's gaze catches mine one last time before I make it out the door and it looks like he wants to say something to me... but he doesn't. Instead he turns and walks in the opposite direction. Nate calls out that he wants to do something tonight, and I nod. Once we're outside Drake nudges my arm.

"So that must be the elusive stepbrother?"

That word, stepbrother. It makes my skin crawl. "He isn't my stepbrother."

"Yet." He corrects.

As if she read my mind Allie comes to the rescue, "So Drake, are you a senior this year like Jo?"

I flash her a grateful smile. The two of them exchange small talk the entire way to the beach and I am thankful for the chance to be alone with my thoughts.

I have no right to be upset with him for hooking up with Cass. He wasn't mine, and I wasn't his. I have no authority to tell him who he can and can't screw. I could, however, be upset that he'd come to me afterwards like some pathetic back up plan.

My brain won't shut up as we walk towards the shore. It's hard not to let this latest revelation overshadow the kindness he'd shown me last night. If he wants to fuck someone else, then why'd he come home? Why'd he wake me up to show me that he hadn't forgotten my birthday? Why had he kissed me with such tenderness and longing? I have so many questions.

"Jo?" Allie's soft voice brought me away from my racing thoughts.

"Yeah," I respond equally as soft.

"You're playing with fire. I'm only saying that because I care about you, and I know my brother. Just- Just be careful. Okay?"

Fuck.

"I don't know what you're talking about. We're not-"

She holds up one of her tiny hands and then places the other on my shoulder. "You don't have to tell me anything, I understand. I just needed to tell you to be careful. You're a tough one, but he can break even the strongest of them."

You're playing with fire. Her words echoed in my mind the rest of the afternoon.

CHAPTER THIRTEEN

Seeing his black car in the driveway while walking back up to the house makes the butterflies in my stomach go wild.

"I think I got too much sun," Allie complains after peeking underneath her bathing-suit strap.

I catch Drake's eyes lingering on her bare skin for a moment and I nudge him playfully. He rolls his eyes and tries to play it off, but I can tell he's starting to have a little crush on her. You'd think this would spark some sort of jealousy over our history together, but it didn't. What we had was completely platonic, our romps in between the sheets hadn't changed that.

I find Nate and Alec lounging lazily on the living room sofa watching a show about a group of men mining for gold. "This is entertainment?" I ask flatly.

"New girl!" Nate snaps his attention away from the television and onto me. "Hey, this may not be grade A quality programming, but it fills the void as we waited for your return." He winks and I can't stifle the laugh.

"You're ridiculous."

A phone vibrates on the coffee table and Alec picks it up, "We gotta go, Kurt needs a ride." He's addressing Nate and completely avoiding any and all eye contact with me. *Okay.*

Nate looks to me and shrugs and heads out the door. I stand there, waiting for Alec to walk past me. Right when he does, he pauses. His knuckles graze my arm ever so lightly, and he whispers something in my ear that sends chills over every inch of my body. "I didn't fuck Cass."

So, he had heard the conversation from earlier.

"Alec," I breathe out.

His green eyes find mine and there's a hunger in them that pierces me to my core. A boyish grin washes over his face and he winks at me. He fucking winks at me, mimicking what Nate had done only moments before.

"We're coming back here tonight, see you then."

With that he's gone, and my feet are cemented to the floor... heart pounding. I finally release the breath that I wasn't even aware I'd been holding.

"JoJo?" Drake calls from the kitchen.

"Uh, yeah. Coming." I gather myself and join them.

Allie is biting into a juicy strawberry and Drake is looking at me like I have three heads. "Dude, what's up with you? Your face is about as red as that strawberry." He gestures to the ripe fruit in between Allie's lips.

"Nothing, I'm fine." I lie.

"Yeah, Okay. And I'm the Queen of England." He retorts in a terrible British accent.

That's his go-to line, and as cliche as it is, it always makes me smile. There's something about picturing my best friend in a dress rocking the crowned jewels that's hard not to laugh at.

I curtsy, "Your Majesty."

"Whatever, I'll leave it alone."

Bullet dodged, at least where Drake was concerned. Allie on the other hand... Let's just say the look on her face made it very clear this conversation was not over.

I attempt to regain control of the situation. "Alec mentioned they were coming back here tonight, I'm guessing to the boat house. Maybe we can all hang out?"

Drake shrugs in a non-committal way and looks to Allie for confirmation.

"Sure, if I don't invite my friends he may let me hang out."

That seems as good a plan as any. I want her to be there, even if she'd be staring daggers at me after every interaction with her brother.

"Jo, help me with something really quick?" She asks, nodding towards the stairs.

Shit.

"Uh, sure."

"Drake, we will just be a sec." She smiles at him sweetly and he returns it. He's completely oblivious and digging into the strawberries she'd set out.

"Spill." She demands once we were inside my room.

I bite the inside of my mouth, trying to figure out what the fuck I'm about to say.

"Well, I don't really know what to spill Allie... I'm so confused right now. Alec, he's- well he's screwing with my head."

She looked exasperated. "He does that. Elaborate?"

"Uh, I feel really awkward telling you this. We seem to be- well we seem to be attracted to each other." I finally get the words out. "Like, a lot. Very attracted to each other."

Allie scrunches up her face in disgust, "Why?"

"I have no clue, but if you figure it out please let me know." I say, plopping down onto the bed. "I know he isn't a nice guy, and I know there is no hearts and flowers with him. Even worse, I also know that his father is about to marry my mother. I have no clue what is wrong with me."

As much as I'd been dreading having this conversation with anyone but my bathroom mirror, it's amazing to finally get it off my chest. She joined me on the bed and placed her palm against my shoulder.

"Jo, I don't know what has happened between you two behind closed doors and to be honest I have no desire to. You are right and wrong about him. He can be a nice guy, he *used* to be a nice guy. He went through some things... some things that he shouldn't have had to deal with alone."

Nate's words echo in my mind as she speaks.

"When our mom died... it hit him the hardest. Maybe even harder than dad. Alec never accepted her fate, he always believed that somehow she'd end up beating it- that she'd be the miracle you always hear about when it comes to terminal cancer patients."

The lump in my throat is rising.

"You're right about the other part though, he doesn't do hearts and flowers. I don't know if he ever will. I won't say my brother can't love because that isn't true. He loves so fiercely that when things fall apart it shatters him. I know he is capable of that kind of love still, I just don't know that he will ever make himself vulnerable enough to feel it again."

There are tears in her eyes now. "Allie, I don't mean to bring up these feelings for you. I'm sorry. I shouldn't have-"

"Look, Jo. I like you, and I want this to work. For all of us. My dad is really happy, and I think your mom is too. If they knew about whatever is happening between you and Alec things would get really weird really fast. Just promise me you won't risk messing everything up to be another one of his conquests. You are better than that. He can be charming, and God knows I love my brother. I love him more than anything in the world- but I also know that he wants to stop this wedding from happening."

The realization of what she's trying to say hits me like a brick wall.

"Please don't be angry at me for saying this, but hasn't a single part of you wondered if this is his plan to stop them from getting married? If it got out that you two were fooling around... it would be the scandal to end all scandals. Especially around here, in this small town? People would never stop talking about it. Dad's career could be seriously damaged. Step-sibling affair? Imagine what that would do to your mom."

I want to tell her that she is way out of line, that he would never do that to our parents. But would he? The truth is I barely knew Alec Miller. I have no clue how far he'd go to get what he wants.

She continues, "He's not a monster, but he's got a damaged heart. I just don't want to watch this all blow up around us."

My heart hurt, as in physical pain shooting through my chest. Is this all a game to him? Am I just another pawn helping him get his check-mate?

I need answers, but the only way that's going to happen is to have a very serious conversation with someone whose heart is locked up tight like a fortress.

No matter how tonight goes, I have a feeling I'm about to open up Pandora's box.

CHAPTER FOURTEEN

The sound of Alec and his friends arriving outside makes it hard to focus on the documentary we were watching in the living room. They never came inside, instead heading straight down the pathway towards the boat house.

"Does your dad just not give a shit about him having people over?" Drake asks, addressing Allie.

She shrugs and answers nonchalantly, "Dad doesn't really mess with Alec much."

I knew this is because he probably holds some intense guilt over checking out when his wife was dying and leaving his son to handle the heavy shit.

"Must be nice." Drake mutters under his breath.

If only he knew just how deep the wounds ran around here.

"So are we going out there?" This time Allie was looking to me for an answer.

I'm not sure what I want to do. I want to face Alec, but this conversation isn't exactly one I can have in front of everyone. We could always stay here, watch documentaries and eat pizza rolls... put off the inevitable.

"New girl!" Nate's voice yelled into the house. I turn and his head is poking through the open back door. "Get out here, you're my partner for beer pong."

Well, I guess that solves this dilemma.

"Looks like we're going out there." I say to Allie and Drake.

My mom and Sean have been locked up in their bedroom since they got home from dinner, no doubt spending *'quality time together'*. Mom has never been the overbearing type, but since moving here, her parenting has been straight up nonexistent. I know it's only because she's stuck in her little bubble with her future husband, but damn.

On the deck, there's now a fold-out table equipped with two groups of red solo cups shaped like pyramids. I join Nate at one side and try not to make it obvious that I'm looking for Alec. Opposite of us is Conner and V, and I can tell they'd already been drinking for a while. I'm definitely the most sober in this crowd, except for Drake and Allie who'd disappeared into the boat house.

"Don't let me down, Jo. I'm counting on you!" Nate says as I prepare to throw the small white ball towards the cups. He's letting me do most of the drinking to play catch up, and the more buzz I get, the better my aim seems to be.

Conner waves his arms in front of the remaining cup trying to distract me to no avail.

"Score!" I yell when the ball falls in.

Nate throws me over his shoulder and does a victory lap around the yard, and I laugh harder than I think I ever have before. When he finally releases me, I notice Alec leaning against the door frame, his eyes on me. Wearing his signature black skinny jeans with holes at the knees and a loose fitting black tank he looks hot. Really hot. The ink that covers his skin is just the icing on the perfectly delicious cake. The heat rises to my cheeks, and other parts of my body. The instinctual reaction I have being in the same general vicinity as him is cruel and unusual punishment. All I want to do is pull him back inside and let him have his way with me, but that's pretty much out of the question at the moment. No, instead I have to keep my distance which is pure torture.

"Round two?" Nate calls out to me as he races back to the table.

"Sure, why not?" I answer back, looking forward to downing a bit more liquid courage before my talk with Alec.

We ran the table all night long, easily becoming the undefeated champions. "What other secret talents are you hiding under there?" Nate teases, hooking his finger underneath my t-shirt.

Oh.

"Um, none really. Beginner's luck, I think." I'd played before, but in the past had been average at best. "Maybe it was just a great partner."

That put a smile on his face. It was hard not to fixate on Nate's smile. It was warm and genuine, the kind of smile that made you feel like none of your problems existed. He was a good looking guy, but his personality took it to the next level. Not many guys looked like him *and* were so fucking nice.

"Pretty sure I'm the lucky one." Suddenly, there's something new in his eyes. Nate and I have had several little moments, but they've mostly stayed in the platonic safe-zone. He takes his thumb and gently brushes it across my cheek, causing the hair along my arms and back of my neck to stand. "You're something else, you know that?"

"What do you mean?" I ask with a shaky voice.

He lets out a breath. "You are so much different than the girls around here, it's refreshing." He takes in my oversized Nirvana tee and leggings. "Look around, all these other girls try so hard to get our attention... and instead all eyes are on you."

I scan the people scattered around the yard. The girls are all dressed to turn heads in tight clothes and heavy makeup.

"I don't think all eyes are on me, Nate. That's sweet though."

He takes a step towards me, "Well mine are. Have been since that night at Shooter's."

There's not enough space between us anymore. As right as this *should* feel, I can't help but pull back.

I don't even need to look to sense his presence. His eyes are zeroing in on us like a laser. "Are you really trying to fuck with her, man?"

Alec's accusation makes me jump.

"What is your problem? I get that you're pissed your dad's getting married but back off Miller." Nate fires back at him and protectively takes a step in front of me.

Alec's eyes lock onto mine and I'm frozen. "Jo, go inside."

"Are you serious? You aren't her keeper. I don't know what has been up with you lately, but you need to get a fucking grip." Nate is not backing down. "Who do you think you are ordering her around?"

I look away from them and realize mostly everyone is staring. *Great, just great.*

"Hey, both of you... chill out. Okay? I'll go."

Nate stares at me in disbelief, "You are not going to let him tell you what to do, Jo. Fuck that."

"She isn't interested, Nate. Take the hint. Jo, just go." Alec grits through clenched teeth.

I need to get out of here before something bad happens, I need to diffuse this situation. Just as I take the first step, Nate shoves Alec, hard. He stumbles back, but it only takes a second or two for him to regain his footing.

"What the hell is going on?" Allie runs to my side.

"I- I don't know. Just help me calm them down, please." I plead, and she shakes her head in frustration when she sees her brother launch towards his best friend.

"Alec! Stop, just walk away." She reaches out for him but he pulls away and slams his fist into Nate's jaw.

Conner, Nash, and Kurt come barreling towards the boys trying to rip them apart. Nash finally gets a grip on Nate with the help of Drake. This allows Conner and Kurt to pull Alec away from him and off towards the boat house.

Allie grabs my hand, "I think we should go."

I nod, and follow her up to the house. As we near the door I hear Alec yelling, "Stay away from her. Stay the fuck away from her."

Drake closes the door behind us and looks at me with a million questions in his eyes. "JoJo, what was that?"

I can't get a word out before the door opens and Alec stumbles inside. His wild eyes stare into me, causing my breath to hitch. "I told everyone to get the fuck out of here."

"Probably a good call. What the hell, Alec? Nate is your best friend." Allie says to her brother, but his gaze doesn't move from mine. After a few seconds of silence he turns and disappears down the stairs into the basement.

"Alright then, Asshole." She mutters.

It seems like Drake is finally beginning to grasp what has transpired outside. Slowly, but surely, he's putting the pieces together. He reaches for my chin and forces me to look into his eyes. "Please tell me this isn't what it looks like. You're not *with* him, right?"

I can't lie to him, not to Drake. "I don't know what we are."

"Jesus, Jo. What are you doing? Your parents are getting married, and he's clearly unhinged."

It takes everything within me to not let the tears pricking at my eyes begin to fall. "He's not- It's not-" I can't get the words to come out.

Allie wraps an arm around me, "Let's not talk about it anymore tonight."

I nod, and Drake lets out an exasperated breath. "Whatever, but we are finishing this tomorrow. Okay?"

I nod again, saying nothing. Instead, I look towards the stairway and know that my mind is already made up. Allie must see it on my face because she takes Drake's hand in her own and asks him to go upstairs with her to watch a movie. He doesn't protest, and once they are out of sight I cross the kitchen and make my way down to Alec.

CHAPTER FIFTEEN

"Alec?" My voice is barely above a whisper but it seems to echo down here. The lights are off, and I immediately trip over something on his floor. "Dammit."

The lamp on his bedside table turns on. He looks disheveled, upset. His lip is swollen and I can see the faint beginnings of a black eye. "Jesus, are you okay?"

I want to touch him, touch his face... be here for him. I'm afraid to though. I am afraid that I don't know what his reaction will be, I don't even know if he wants me down here.

"I'm fine." His response is clipped.

I run through a few different scenarios in my mind and try to figure out the right words to say.

"Jo?"

I look up at him and his eyes seem so conflicted.

"Yes?"

He holds up his hand, and when I take it he pulls me onto the bed with him. It's too intimate which only confuses me more. I let my head settle onto his chest, and the sound of his heartbeat instantly relaxes me.

"Why did you do that?" I ask him quietly.

He waits a few seconds before answering, "I don't know."

"You don't know why you started a fight with your best friend or why you pulled me into bed with you?" I press, praying that he doesn't flip the switch and turn cold again.

"No, I don't know why."

I don't believe that, but I'm scared if I keep pushing him he'll just shut me out.

"Okay." I concede.

We lay there in silence for a while, neither of us daring to be the first to speak again. His chest rising and falling underneath me is intoxicating, and I know that if I don't leave soon I'll fall asleep here in his bed.

"I need to go."

His grip on me tightens. "Don't."

These simple sentences and one word responses are driving me insane. I tilt my head up to face him, "Alec, talk to me. What was that out there?"

His jaw tenses. I know he doesn't want to do this, he doesn't want to talk. I need him to though, I need him to let me in. I need to understand what's happening between us. "Please?"

"You are exhausting." He finally says, and I can't help the small giggle that escapes my lips.

"Me? Seriously?"

He shifts, "Yes, you." His thumb begins to trace my bottom lip. "You're driving me mad."

He had to know that the feeling is mutual. This thing, whatever the hell it is... is driving me mad too. "Alec, what are we doing? There's no scenario where this ends well, for either of us."

Rolling away from me he stares at the ceiling. "I know that. I don't know why I can't stay away from you. I planned on hating you, making you miserable." A small smirk appears on his face, "...clearly that isn't working out so well for me."

I let out another giggle, "Can't say I'm upset you've abandoned the plan to make my life a living hell."

Hearing him admit that he planned on running me off, brings

Allie's warning from earlier back into my mind. "I need to ask you something, and I need for you to be honest. Okay?"

Alec nods.

"Are you- fuck I don't know how to say this." I take a deep breath and try again. "You aren't using me to get to our parents, right? This isn't some Hail Mary to have the wedding cancelled?"

He sits up and locks his eyes on mine. "What?"

God, he's mad. "I know you don't want your dad to marry my mom, and I also know that a scandal between their children could ruin him. In his line of work reputation is everything... it may even be enough to make him cancel the wedding to avoid the risk."

Alec seems shocked that I've put so much thought into this. I decide to leave out his sister's involvement in planting the seeds.

"I just- I don't know what's happening but it feels like it could be something big. It feels different than any other relationship I've been in. I need to know if this is real." I suck in a breath and await his response, which seems like it takes hours to come.

His fingers rake through his dark hair as he stares at me through narrowed eyes. "Relationship?"

"Fuck, Alec. I say all that and the only thing you hear is that word? Jesus. Relationships aren't kryptonite, the word can't hurt you." Frustration pulses through me and I just want to shake this beautifully broken man. "Yes, relationship. The connection between two concepts... objects... people."

"Jo," he breathes out my name and I know that I'd give anything to hear him keep saying it. "I don't want them to get married, you're right about that. I haven't hid that from you or anyone else. I planned on hating you... avoiding you. Isolating you so that you felt alone here. I never planned on wanting you. Wanting you so bad that I can't control myself. You've gotten under my skin and I can't shake it. You confuse me, infuriate me, and make me crazy."

I suck in a sharp breath.

"You challenge me, tease me... make me want you without even trying. I've never met a girl like you. I've spent every second since you've arrived counting the reasons we can't do this, why I can't do this with you."

I meet his hard gaze, "Tell me."

"What?"

"Tell me the reasons... maybe it'll help me walk out of this room. Tell me all of the reasons we can't do this. Convince me to leave right now and not look back." I try to feign conviction with my voice, but it's so hard.

His face looks pained, like saying these things out loud is physically painful.

"We are about to be step-siblings. Your mother is marrying my father, and I don't think that there is anything we can do to change that. I'm older... not by much, but you are still in high school. I've graduated, work full-time, and have already lived a harder life than most. You are young and haven't experienced anything of the world."

I want to object, but I need him to keep talking. I need to hear this.

"We would have to lie to everyone, no one could ever know. This- what's happening now? It would always be like this. Secret meetings when everyone is asleep, sneaking around behind the backs of everyone you care about. A sinful and corrupt affair that nobody else would understand. Fuck, even if we weren't about to be related by marriage they would never approve. Look at me, and look at you. I have a reputation that follows me around like a second shadow, I've done horrible things. You? You are-"

"I'm no angel, Alec." I try to touch his face but he pulls away.

"It doesn't matter if you aren't an angel, I'm still the tattooed bad-boy devil that no mother wants to see walk through the door on her daughter's arm."

I know he's right about that part. There's no way our families would approve of us together, especially not my mother.

"The biggest reason is that I know at the end of this you'll hate me, and to be honest, I don't think I could handle that. It's crazy, before you came all I wanted was for you to hate me- to despise me. And now? I think if you actually hated me it would break me. I didn't think there was anything left to break, but if there is...that would do it."

Why would I hate him?

I grab his hand, and this time he allows it. "Alec, why do you think I would hate you?"

His hand finds my cheek and I close my eyes, internally swooning over his touch.

"Because of this." He says quietly.

I open my eyes and furrow my brows in confusion, "I don't understand."

"You crave something that I am not capable of giving. I can touch you, kiss you, fuck you to your heart's desire, but I will never love you. Not the way you want me to. I don't think I have that inside me to give. You are going to want more from me, and when I can't live up to those expectations you'll hate me for it. When I disappoint you... I just-"

I silence him with my lips, lacing my fingers together behind his neck. He tries to fight it, but can't. His lips open for me and the kiss deepens. When we pull apart, foreheads pressed together I can sense the confused look on his face.

"Alec, you don't give yourself enough credit. You've convinced yourself that you are a shell of a man, but that is so far from the truth. You feel, and you feel deeply. That's why you moved back home to take care of your mom and sister, and also why you are so mad at your father. After that night in the boat house you lied to our parents for me, told them that the Jeep's battery died so I wouldn't have to answer any uncomfortable questions. You did that because you care. My birthday... that gesture was incredible. Loveless men don't do things like that. And that fight with Nate? You were jealous... because seeing him with me drove you mad. It's because you care about me."

I take a deep breath before finishing, "And what you just said to me? About not wanting to do this because you think I will end up hating you? The fact that disappointing and hurting me affects you in such a profound way- it proves that you are more than capable of giving love."

Alec looks at me, wonder in his eyes. He looks so much younger in this moment than he ever has before.

"I don't think you truly believe that you aren't capable of giving love, I think the problem is that you don't think you deserve that same love in return."

I press my lips to his cheek, and then relax into his hard body.

"But you couldn't be more wrong, Alec Miller."

CHAPTER SIXTEEN

The next few days have been a blur. Stealing kisses when no one is around and sneaking about when everyone's asleep... it's exhilarating. Knowing that at any moment we could be found out makes each encounter dangerous and explosive. Alec's black eye is almost healed, but each night I press my lips to the bruises and kiss them away. I've avoided Nate and dodged all of Allie's questions that have anything to do with the incident that day by the dock. She's been so consumed with texting and FaceTiming Drake to bother with it too much, which is a blessing in disguise for Alec and I.

As happy as I am for them, I can't help but feel the tiniest twinge of envy when Allie talks about how incredible he is or shares their plans for the next time he comes to visit. It has nothing to do with wanting him for myself, but the simple fact is, that they don't have to hide their relationship. They can talk on the phone, plan dates, and post pictures publicly without the fear of any backlash. Us? That's a big negative ghost-rider. If anyone found out about me doing the Pink Panther walk down to Alec's room every night, they would have nothing positive to say, and that's putting it mildly.

"Josephine, we need to go! I can't miss my fitting, sweetie!" My mother yells from downstairs as I take in my reflection in the mirror one last time. I've opted for a pair of white high-waisted shorts and a light grey knotted tee. Its casual, but still stylish.

"Coming, Mom!" I call back to her and slip on my white tennis shoes. We're headed downtown for her final wedding dress fitting. The big day is fast approaching and planning has been thrown into overdrive. Today it'll just be us, and to be honest I'm looking forward to spending some quality time with her. We've both been so caught up in our own lives since moving here that there hasn't been much one-on-one interaction. It's been just me and her for the longest time, it feels foreign that we've drifted so far in such a short time frame.

"Are you excited to see the final result?" I ask her, and her smile is endearing.

"Excited, yes... but also so nervous. I've been terrified that all this stress-eating is going to catch up to me and the back won't zip. I think I've had that nightmare three times this week."

I can't help but laugh. My mother is beautiful, and has had a small frame for as long as I can remember. She could stand to put on a few pounds, and even then she would still have a body that women her age pay lots of money for.

"Mom, you're hot. You're going to knock everyone's socks off when you walk down the aisle, especially Sean." I clasp my hand around hers and she gives it a squeeze.

I can tell by the slight reddening of her cheeks, that she appreciates the boost of confidence. "Thank you, I needed that."

At the bridal boutique, the sales associate leads my mother into a curtained off dressing room and helps her into the dress. I'm seated on a plush bench and pick at my cuticles as I wait for the big unveiling. When the associate comes out of the dressing room, she's beaming. "Just wait until you see her, it's perfect."

The curtain opens and when she steps out I can't stifle the sudden surge of emotion that washes over me like a tidal wave. "Oh my God, mom. You look amazing."

The dress is fitted to her body all the way down to her calves where it begins to fan out, creating the perfect mermaid silhouette.

The associate has also pinned up Mom's hair and clipped in a simple yet elegant veil that drapes over her shoulders. The lace overlay is classically southern, and I wonder if our new home had anything to do with that stylistic choice. There's the smallest amount of beading around the sweetheart neckline, and then again towards the bottom interwoven with the mermaid tail hemline.

"Seriously, Mom. It's incredible. You're glowing." I manage to say, and she's crying while taking in the scene in the large mirror.

"I'm so happy, Josephine. So very happy. This new life here... It's everything I could have dreamed of and more."

Great. Now on top of the blubbering caused by how beautiful my mom looks in her dress, there's now added tears from the guilt I feel for sneaking around with Alec.

Nope. Do not feel guilty. You aren't doing anything wrong. You are simply exploring your feelings for him in private because the circumstances are less than ideal. They wouldn't understand... no one will understand.

———

When we arrive back home I run up the stairs taking them two at a time, eager to plug in my phone that has been dead now for over an hour. I was texting Alec when it died and apparently my mother is the one human on the planet who doesn't keep a charger in her car. When I close the door behind me and turn around, I immediately let out a gasp and jump backwards.

"Jesus, what the hell are you doing in here?" I bark out somewhere in between a yell and a whisper.

He smirks and shrugs one of his shoulders, "You didn't respond and I didn't know when you'd be back. I'm heading out for the night but wanted to see you before I left."

Oh. A smile tugs at my lips.

"My phone died and mom didn't have a charger. Where are you off to?" I ask, trying not to sound too needy.

Alec grabs for my hand and pulls me into his lap. "Guy's night, nothing special. I'll probably crash there though." He nuzzles his face into my neck and begins to strategically place kisses in all of the places that make my body go weak and my breath go ragged.

"Crash there?" I say and instantly wish the words would have stayed inside my brain. It's obvious that I am disappointed and don't want him to leave.

He pulls away and examines my face clearly looking for some explanation as to why I am being weird all the sudden, "Yeah? I don't want to drive after drinking all night."

I force a smile and nod as if it all makes sense now. "Of course. Well, have a good time. Don't get into too much trouble."

His face softens again and the little smirk is back. "Nah, it'll be a chill night. Plus, I'm sure it'll be hard to have too much fun when I think of you being here in this big bed all alone."

He always does this... turns every conversation into a flirty innuendo that leads to a steamy make-out session. The only difference is that right now it's still daylight... and our families are just down the stairs. It would be so easy for someone to walk in right now- to catch us in the act. My eyes dart towards the door and as if he reads my mind he lets out an exasperated sigh.

"Yeah yeah, bad idea. I know."

I place a palm against his cheek and kiss him before rising from his lap, putting the necessary space between us.

He stalks towards the door and grabs the knob before turning back to face me, "I'll miss you tonight." He says with a wink, and then he's gone. I sink into the bed and let out an audible groan.

I remember my dead as a doornail phone and roll over to plug it in. When it comes back to life a few notifications begin to buzz against the nightstand.

A text from Veronica catches me off guard, and I slide to unlock my phone. I haven't seen her since the incident a few nights ago.

V: Girl's night. You in?

Well, that's certainly interesting.

Jo: What do you have planned?

The three dots signifying she is typing pop up immediately.

V: I'm thinking the docks. The guys are at a party tonight

and decided none of the girls were invited, some bullshit about needing some man-time.

I laugh remembering how Alec tried to play it off as a chill night with the guys.

V: If they want to ditch us for God knows what, we should do the same. ;)

Okay, this is tempting. I look at my bed and then back to the phone. Do I want to stay in? If I stay in, will I think about Alec all night and wish he was downstairs waiting on me to sneak into his bed when everyone is asleep? Or will I go full-blown crazy pants and worry that he is with another girl?

V: Don't overthink it, Carpe that Diem girl.

Okay, can she read my mind?

Jo: I'm in.

Carpe fucking Diem.

CHAPTER SEVENTEEN

In thirty minutes, I've fully transformed myself into a new person. My hair is pulled into a high power-ponytail and my makeup is on the darker side. I'm rocking a tight pair of denim skinny jeans and a black crop top that hits at the perfect spot, showing just the right amount of skin. I slide on an army green bomber jacket for now, deciding against giving the family downstairs a complete heart attack when I walk out the door. I look hot, and that isn't a compliment I often give to myself.

My phone buzzes.

V: Here.

Alright, it's game time.

I pull on my docs and head down the stairs, calling out to Mom that I am going out with a friend.

"A friend? Who?" She asks as she turns the corner.

"Her name is Veronica, she's going to be a senior with me this year." I answer, pulling the jacket around my midriff.

"Oh! You've made a girlfriend! That's great. What time will you be home?"

Good question...

"I'm not really sure. We're having a girl's night, so whatever normally happens there will determine that." I laugh awkwardly, and mom gives me a reassuring smile. She knows I've never really had girlfriends before, and I know she's happy that I'm getting to experience it now.

"Just keep your phone on you and update me on your plans, I don't want to worry all night."

I hug her briefly before darting for the door.

"Damnnnn, Caliente!" Veronica howls out the window as I approach the car. I shake my hips and do a twirl soaking up the compliments. There's another girl I don't recognize sitting in the passenger seat, and V introduces her as Macy. Her deep skin is stunning, and it contrasts perfectly with the white jersey dress she is wearing.

"So the docks?" I ask while sliding into the back seat.

"Yeah, should be a good crowd there tonight." V responds.

She turns up the stereo and blares music the entire ride, and when Macy passes me a wine cooler I take it without a second thought.

Carpe Diem. That's my motto tonight. I will not stress over Alec, I will not wonder what he is doing. I am not *that girl* who goes loony toons when the guy she likes goes off on his own for the night.

"Damn, Jules looks hot tonight." Macy says as we exit the car and walk towards the crowd.

I follow her eyes and see a girl dancing with a red solo cup in her hand. Her movements are slow and seductive, and when her eyes meet Macy's she dials it up a few extra notches.

"Yeah, I'm on that like white on rice." She says playfully and walks over to join the dancing girl.

V wraps an arm around me and laughs, "She has more game than any guy I know, that's for sure. Drives the ladies crazy!"

That doesn't surprise me in the least. Macy exudes confidence, and not to mention she's gorgeous. She's so smooth as she flirts, and Jules effectively becomes putty in her hands.

"Damn, you're right about that. What did that take? Three minutes?" I ask, half joking and half impressed by how quickly Macy worked. Their bodies are now grinding to the music, and I smile.

At least one of us may get laid tonight.

V grabs my hand and leads me towards a few kegs and pours me a beer. "So, see anything that catches your eye?" She asks mischievously.

Anything that catches my eye? "What?"

"Come on girl, see anything you like? Any man candy?"

Oh, right. Now this, I hadn't thought about. Of course she'd think I'm single. I can't exactly tell her who I'm really interested in.

I have clearly taken too long to respond and she nudges me playfully. "I mean, you are single. There are plenty of hotties around here tonight. Might as well have a little fun."

Am I single? Alec and I hadn't exactly defined whatever it is that we are. I mean, I sure as hell hadn't thought of being with anyone else…but had he? We still hadn't slept together. Could I really expect him to not want to sleep with anyone when he wasn't getting that from me? It wasn't like I didn't want to…we just hadn't really gotten there yet.

"Uhm, yeah. I guess I am single- I just don't really think I'm looking for anything right now." I respond, trying to sound sure of myself.

"Hey, no pressure. Let's just see how the night goes. Deal?"

I smile back at her, "Deal."

A few hours later I'm buzzed and happy. The music is still thumping loudly, and V is at my side moving and swaying with me. There'd been a few brave souls to approach me for a dance, but I'd waved them all off without interest just as quickly as they came. I couldn't help it. None of them could even hold a candle to Alec. His large frame, those hard muscles, and God those tattoos? There was no way your typical run of the mill high school boy could compare to that.

"Hold on, it's Connor." V says holding up her ringing phone to show me the screen. She picks up and starts shoving through the crowd trying to find a quiet place to hear what he has to say. As soon as I'm alone a guy approaches me and asks if I need a refill.

"I'm Caleb." He says with a friendly voice and a smile. He's handsome, but in a more conventional way. Not in the Rebel Without a Cause way like Alec. His blonde hair and blue eyes paired with tan skin make him look like the stereotypical jock that is the lead in every chick-flick teen romantic comedy.

"Sure, thanks. I'm Jo." I answer back, deciding he looks nice enough. Plus, I'm thirsty. He leaves with my cup and returns a few moments later with it full to the brim.

"Are you new? I don't recognize you." Caleb asks, and I nod.

"I just moved here, I start school at Southside in the fall. Senior year." I reply.

"Me too. Well, it's nice to meet you Jo. Cool name, by the way." Caleb flashes another smile and then turns around fading back into the crowd about the same time that V returns.

"Everything okay with Connor?" I ask her when she's close enough that I don't have to yell over the music.

"Oh, yeah! Of course. He just wanted to check in. I told him we we're having a girl's night. He says hello."

"What are they up to?" I ask cryptically.

"You know, the usual. Strip clubs and cheap hookers." The look on my face must convey pure horror, and she bursts out into a fit of laughter. "Kidding, only kidding. You should have seen your face, girl. They are at Billiards & Barstools. It's a bar for playing pool, they go every so often and have tournaments. Lots of friendly competition and betting going on, I'm sure."

I instantly feel better about Alec's plans, and can't help but smile. "Oh, well that sounds like fun."

V shrugs, "I guess. They seem to enjoy it. It's pretty boring for me though. I've only gone a few times." I watch as she pulls out her phone again and squints at the screen. Her fingers type out a message but before she can put it away it rings again.

"What the-" She says, clearly confused by the message.

"What is it?" I ask, immediately concerned.

"Well, on the phone I mentioned that you were with me at the docks. I guess Connor told the guys when he got back inside."

"And?" I ask, not quite understanding where this is going.

She hands me her phone so that I can read the messages.

Connor: Missin you, have fun.

Connor: You said Jo is with you, right?

V: Yeah, why?

I raise an eyebrow, still not understanding. She taps the back button to take me back to her inbox. I see Alec's name signaling an incoming message.

Alec: You took Jo to the docks?

Alec: Wtf is she doing?

My stomach drops and I look up to meet V's gaze. She's eyeing me with a mixture of confusion and amusement. V takes back the phone and begins to respond to Alec.

V: Having a good time, what's it to you?

She winks at me, "That'll make him stew." I can tell she thinks it's humorous that he's so worried about what I'm up to, but I'm also pretty sure that she thinks he's asking to be a dick. That he's upset with her for bringing his enemy across the battle lines. Oh, how wrong she is.

Alec: Are you drinking?

"Seriously? Does he think he's your dad?" V scoffs. I know she's had a good bit to drink, we both have... and it seems like the liquid courage is making her feisty.

V: Chill out, Alec. She's in good hands. I won't let anything happen to your stepsister. You know me better than that.

"There, I was nice. Now let's dance." She puts the phone on silent and slides it back into her pocket, and I instantly regret leaving mine in the car. I have a sinking feeling in the pit of my stomach that I can't place, but the more I think about it I know she's right. I am having a good time, and I'm not doing anything wrong. I down another cup of beer before falling into place with her amid the growing crowd of bodies grinding to the music.

CHAPTER EIGHTEEN

My feet have started to hurt from all the dancing, but I'm having so much fun that I don't even care. V is having a blast too, and now Macy and Jules are at our side. We've formed a sort of circle and are all swaying and moving with each other, not even aware of the others dancing around us.

Someone brushes against me and I turn to see Caleb, the Mr. Nice Guy from earlier. He's noticeably more intoxicated now, which means he's also much more confident in his approach with me. "Hey there again, Jo right?"

I nod, and he smiles. "How about another refill?" He asks, but I politely decline. The world has been spinning for a while now, so I think another beer is the last thing I need.

V sends a wink my way and gives a nod of approval. She clearly thinks I need to be giving boy wonder here a shot, but I can't help but think of Alec. I don't want the clean-cut easy choice, I want the messy and complicated shit show with my villain. I want the chaos.

"You sure? You look thirsty." Caleb tries again, but before I can politely reject him again a deep voice handles it for me.

"She said no thanks, now run along."

Caleb's eyes widen and without another word he turns and walks away. I look up and see Alec towering over me with a look on his face that I can only describe as pure possessiveness.

"What the hell? What are you doing here?" V shrieks. About that time, Connor appears behind Alec and shrugs at her, making it obvious he has no clue why they are there either.

We're having an entire conversation with our eyes, no words necessary. His ask me what I'm doing here, and why I didn't tell him I was coming. Mine answer that it was last minute, and that I didn't want to interrupt his guys' night. Alec sighs and tenses his jaw. His eyes shift, and I know he's asking me if I want to leave. I nod.

I turn to face V and she is eyeing me intently, brows furrowed. I know there will be a conversation about this little exchange she just witnessed.

"I'm taking Jo home." Alec announces.

V grabs my arm and pulls me to the side. "Dude, what the heck just happened? Are you guys suddenly telepathic? That was weird. Are you sure you want to leave with him? I can take you-"

I cut her off and wrap her in a hug. "I had so much fun tonight, but I really do need to get home. Text me tomorrow? We can talk then, okay?"

She seems to accept this, for now. "Sure... as long as you are cool with leaving with him."

I nod, reassuring her that I am fine.

I follow Alec to the car and realize I couldn't care less about the confused looks on his friend's faces. Instead I feel triumphant. He wanted me, he left them to come get me. He wanted me all for himself. The thought alone gets me hot, and I count down the moments until we are finally alone.

The car is silent as we pull away from the docks, and the lights fade into the darkness the farther we drive. I don't know what to say to break the tension.

"So did you win?" I finally ask.

"What?"

"Pool. V said y'all were at a billiards club. Did you win?"

I can see the smile on his lips, "I was doing alright, but then I was distracted."

Oh really. "You don't say? What caused that to happen?" I ask innocently.

His knuckles are turning white and I know he's gripping the steering wheel for dear life. "I found out my girl was at some party, no doubt being swarmed by other men."

My girl.

I still, completely unable to move-to breathe.

"I figured it was a smart decision to go scoop her up before someone better came along and made a more appealing offer." He continues, and I try to will myself to resume regular respiratory rhythms. "I'm glad I did too. There's no reason she should look that fucking hot without me around."

My heart is pounding, and I'm convinced he can hear it from the driver's seat.

"She's glad you decided to come get her, too. Those other guy's offers weren't nearly as appealing...not by a long shot." I say, my voice unintentionally low and husky. The need I have for him right now is all consuming, and I need relief. "In fact, she thinks you should pull over and show her exactly how glad you are to see her."

I am surprised by my forwardness, but at this point I'm past being embarrassed. I just need him to satisfy this ache.

"No." He growls.

"What?" I cry out. There's no way he's going to reject me right now, is there?

"I'm not fucking you for the first time in a car. It'll be in my bed, where I can do everything I want to do to you without being cramped or rushed."

Oh.

His hands tighten on the steering wheel again and I worry that he may just rip it right off. He's aching too, I can feel it.

When we pull up to the house and make it inside, the tension between us is so thick I can barely stand it. There's a slight awkwardness because we both know what's about to happen, but the excitement overshadows it two-fold. He holds out his hand and leads me downstairs quietly, and my heart races as we get closer and closer to his bed.

I barely have time to sit on the edge of the bed before his lips crash into mine. The kiss is reckless and full of raw passion, causing my lips to open for his instinctively. A jolt of electricity races throughout me when his hands begin to explore my body, everything within me coming alive- building and building with anticipation for what is to come.

"God, you taste so sweet." He murmurs into my mouth, and I want to melt into the bed. Our bodies begin to move in sync with one another creating a deliciously perfect friction that leaves me wanting more, needing more.

I move to straddle him and his impressive length strains against those tight black pants that I've grown to love so much. His hardness presses into me, showing me how badly he wants this. "Do you see what you do to me? Can you feel how much I want you?" He kisses me again, this time harder. I let out a moan into his mouth and he flips our position so that he's over me, staring down at me like a starving wild animal going in for the kill.

His hands claw feverishly at my clothing, trying to rip it from my body. I reach down to help him with my pants, and once the button is undone. he pulls them off and tosses them across the room.

"My turn," I say quietly. I run my fingers up his hard stomach savoring each curve and contour. I slowly pull his shirt off, and then let my fingers run against his skin all the way back down until I reach his belt. I press kisses to his chest as I work to remove every single layer that separates him from me.

"Jo, I need to be inside you." He says, voice low and gravelly.

The primal urges I feel right now are unlike anything I have ever experienced. I need to know what it feels like for him to fill me, to be deep inside me.

When his pants are successfully on the ground he tugs down his briefs, and I see his length spring free. He leans over me to pull a condom from his bedside table, and slides it on with ease.

He's no amateur.

His finger wraps around my panties and pulls them down, the cool air hitting me and causing me to shiver. Then, he's over me again. He's at my entrance, slowly sliding up and down- preparing me for the moment that he pushes inside. Our eyes are locked on one another, and if he doesn't put me out of my misery I may combust. Again, as if reading my mind he begins to slowly push into me. With each stroke going deeper and deeper, my moans all the reassurance he needs that it is exactly what I want. I ball my fist up and bite down on it, hard- in an attempt to stifle the pleasure-induced animalistic noises escaping from me. His mouth falls to my ear and he whispers, "I wish you didn't have to do that. I wish I could hear you scream for me."

"I am so close, so close." I gasp, eyes rolling back. I'm consumed with how incredible this feels, with how perfectly he fits with me.

He picks up the pace and I tighten around him. We come apart at the seams together, both covered in sweat and groaning in lust. He collapses against me and I can barely breathe, chest heaving rapidly up and down. He stays inside me for a few more seconds as he steadies himself, and then slowly pulls out of me, making me shudder.

"That was-" I begin,

"Everything." He finishes my thought.

And he's right.

CHAPTER NINETEEN

After what happened last night, there's no turning back as far as I'm concerned. I'm all in. Leaving his bedroom and returning to my own is physically painful, and all I want is to stay wrapped up in his arms until the sun comes up.

The wedding is now two weeks away and it's all hands-on deck for last minute preparations. I've been put in charge of creating a spreadsheet of all the RSVP's and confirming the arrangements for the catering, venue, photographer, and band. Allie volunteered her creative expertise to put together the bouquets and tie hundreds of tiny ribbons onto little bags of birdseed to throw at the happy couple as they make their exit. Alec has stayed as far away from helping as possible, but this didn't really come as a surprise to anyone.

"Sean, passports. Where are they? We need to make sure they are accounted for." My mom says as she frantically paces the kitchen.

"Already taken care of, they're sitting on my desk. Baby, relax. We have everything under control." He wraps his arms around my mother and places a kiss on her temple. "All this stress is going to drive you mad. This is a time to be happy."

I can't help but smile at them. They really do seem to be the perfect match. He's able to calm her crazy which is no small feat. Their honeymoon will be spent on some exotic island far away for an entire week, and while I'm bummed I won't be able to enjoy it... I can't pretend that a week alone with Alec doesn't sound like a dream come true. Sure Allie will be here, but sneaking around behind the back of one person is much easier than three.

I work my way down the 'To Do' list and cross the items off one by one. Everything seems to be in order, which makes me let out a sigh of relief.

"I think this may actually go off without a hitch." I say to Allie, and she smiles.

"I think you may be right." She responds.

Once I'm done making my calls, I shift my efforts to helping her tie up the bags of birdseed until my fingers start to go numb, then I call it quits. She waves me off, and I plop down on the sofa to relax for a bit. I check my messages and see one from Veronica.

V: Hey Houdini, that disappearing act last night was a fun party trick. How about we grab lunch so you can explain what the hell all that was about?

Just great, how am I going to come up with an answer that justifies in any capacity why Alec would leave guy's night, drive across town, and insist on taking me home. Even more, why the hell I went willingly.

Jo: Ha Ha, very funny. There is no great mystery here, I was just tired.

The three dots pop up quickly.

V: Mmmhm, and I'm Miss America. I may have been drunk but I'm def not blind. Something fishy is going on with you and stepbrother dearest.

I cringe at the accusation.

Jo: One, he isn't my stepbrother. Two, nothing fishy is going on. Three, I am actually starving so if you really want to grab lunch that sounds great.

V: Meet me at the deli in fifteen?

I send back the thumbs up emoji and head for the Jeep parked outside.

"Spill it." V demands once we've sat down at the small bistro table in the back corner of the deli.

"There's nothing to tell." I say, but I worry that my reddening face is giving me away.

"Connor said as soon as he mentioned I had taken you to the docks Alec paid off his tab and told them guy's night was over. Then, he shows up and pretty much beats his chest like a gorilla to scare off Caleb. When I first met you things were pretty much the polar opposite between you two... then you leave with him? Come on, something is going on."

I stare at her, my mouth open as I try to think of something- anything to say that won't sound like bullshit.

"Might want to close your mouth before a bug flies in there." V rolls her eyes and laughs. "There's obviously some major chemistry happening under that roof of yours, but don't worry. Your dirty little secret is safe with me." She winks, and I'm stunned.

"It's not- Well you see... It's not that simple." I fumble my words around and V laughs at me again.

"Seriously, chill out. No judgement here. I don't exactly get what you see in him, but it's not my place to have an opinion."

I want to leap across the table and hug her. Hug her for being so *normal* about this.

"He's not the same with me, he's- he's kind... and gentle. He's warm and affectionate. Trust me, when we first met I thought he was the world's biggest asshole. In reality, he's kind of the opposite." I find myself defending him to someone that probably knows him better than I do. She's clearly known him longer, but I have to believe that I know the real Alec Miller better than she does.

"Damn, you've got it bad."

I sigh and bury my face in my hands, "Tell me about it."

"Are you like, dating? Or just roommates with benefits?" V asks, and I shrug.

"To be completely honest, I don't think either of us know what we are, or what we want to come out of this. We almost hooked up the night we met, before we knew who the other one was. That night we figured it out, and we tried to leave what almost happened in the past... it was just too hard. It's like gravity pulls us back towards each other, it's inevitable." As terrified as I am that someone really knows about Alec and I, it feels so good to be able to talk about this to a friend.

"Forbidden love and dark family secrets, sounds very Shakespearean."

I laugh at her little joke, but she kind of has a point. "Let's just hope this story doesn't end up with poison or daggers to the heart."

We finish our salads, and to my surprise V changes the subject to something much less taboo. We discuss her relationship with Connor, the wedding, and of course school. In this moment, I am so thankful for this newfound friendship.

When I get back home Alec's car still isn't in the driveway. That nagging voice in the back of my mind tells me to text him, to find out where he is and ask when he'll be back... but I tell her to get a grip and stay quiet up there.

Instead, I curl up on the sofa in the den and flip through Amazon trying to find something to watch. I settle on Game of Thrones and snuggle up under a blanket. Just as the beginning credits begin to play I hear the front door open and close, and a few seconds later Alec plops down onto the couch at my feet.

"Hey there." He says, making my heart rate instantly skyrocket.

I frantically look towards the door making sure no one is around. "What are you doing?" I ask him, and he smiles.

"There's nothing suspicious about watching TV together, Jo. Just relax."

He's right, there is nothing odd about what is happening. If Mom or Sean walked by it would look totally normal, just two people watching Game of Thrones.

His hand wraps around my calf under the blanket and we watch an intense battle scene in silence. It's nice to do something so normal, something that requires zero sneaking around. Our only secret here is the way his thumb is innocently tracing tiny circles on my leg. You'd think watching a horde of undead corpses attack my favorite characters would be a mood killer, but in reality spending time with Alec like this only makes me want him more.

It makes me happy that he wants to be around me, to just sit in silence with me. It breaks my heart that we can't do things like this more often, and that we can be open about what is happening between us. I'm relieved that Veronica knows about us, that at least I have one person that I can call tomorrow and tell about this moment. It makes me hungry for more... I want more of this. I want more of the stolen kisses and scandalous rendezvous, but I also want more of the normal couple stuff. I want to go on a date, a real date where we don't give a shit who sees us together.

All the various thoughts and emotions flooding my head are exhausting, and it doesn't take long before my eyelids begin to flutter. I let out a yawn, and then a quick kiss is pressed against my cheek.

"Goodnight, Jo." His voice is basically a whisper. He retreats back to his side of the couch and goes back to watching the episode. I know there is a smile on my face as I drift to sleep, and I dream of Alec Miller. I dream of a world where our parents aren't getting married, and where we meet in some totally cliche way with no baggage or unsavory circumstances. It's a classic story of a boy meeting a girl and them both realizing they are crazy for each other.

Sweet Dreams indeed.

CHAPTER TWENTY

I wake up to the sound of the vacuum cleaner and let out a loud groan, cursing whoever is behind the horrible noise.

"Jesus, what time is it?" I grumble, covering my face with the blanket.

"You don't get to complain about being woken up when you sleep in the family room, Josephine."

Mom. I groan again and throw the blanket off my body. "I must've fallen asleep watching TV, sorry."

A flashback of the night before causes me to look down towards the other side of the couch, no Alec. He must've gone back to his room after I passed out.

"What time is it?" I ask her, stretching my arms above my head.

"It's still early, it's only eight. I've been stress cleaning since the sun came up."

I offer her a sympathetic smile, "Please stop stressing so much, it's going to be great. We have crossed all our T's and dotted all our I's."

Mom returns my gesture and shrugs, "Maybe I'll finally be relaxed when it's time to walk down the aisle. Anyways, what are your plans today?"

Good question, as of right now the answer is a whole lot of nothing. "No plans, I kind of want to hit the beach. I may see what Allie is up to."

She nods and tells me to have fun, then goes back to obsessively vacuuming perfectly straight lines into the plush carpet. A giggle escapes my lips as I pass by her, this has always been one of her quirks. I guess there are worse things she could be using as an outlet for stress.

Upstairs I find Allie sprawled out on her bed with headphones in, bopping her head and kicking her feet to the beat. I knock on the door frame and she pulls out on the headphones, "Oh hey!"

"Hey, what are you up to today?" I ask her.

"Other than my daily FaceTime with Drake my plans are nonexistent. You?"

That earns a smile from me. I couldn't be happier that they hit it off so well. "Same here, well minus the video chat with Drake part. Want to go to the beach?"

She nods enthusiastically and we plan on leaving in an hour. When I get back into my bedroom I shoot a quick text to Alec.

Jo: Going to the beach with Allie today, hope to see you later. ;)

I jump in the shower and throw on my bathing suit, deciding on a lavender bikini that still has the tags on it. Before walking downstairs to meet Allie in the kitchen I check my phone again, no response from Alec. That doesn't surprise me though, he's probably still asleep.

We climb into the Jeep and head for the beach, a cooler of waters and sandwiches inside in tow. The plan is to spend most of the day there in hopes to soak up as much Summer sun as possible before school starts back up. Plus, I want as much glow as I can get for the wedding pictures. The weather is perfect and our regular spot is relatively empty. We lay out the towels and spray each other down with tanning lotion.

As the hours pass, we set alarms on our phones so that we remember to flip onto our stomachs and then back over. The last thing either of us needs is to have awkward tan lines from too much sun on one side of our body. The audio-book I'm currently listening to on Audible fills my ears and I'm completely relaxed. This move has turned out to be the farthest thing from a disaster, and I can't wipe the permanent grin off my face.

We pull back up to the house just as the sun begins to lower, leaving the sky an incredible painting of oranges, purples and pinks. I've tried to avoid clicking on my phone every five minutes to check for a response from Alec, but at this point I can't help it. An overwhelming sense of unease has been bubbling for the last hour or so. He should've responded by now, there's no way he's still asleep. Is he okay? Did something happen?

"You okay? You seem really distracted all the sudden." Allie asks as we exit the car.

"Oh, yeah. I'm fine. Just thinking, sorry."

His car isn't here.

Allie must have seen my eyes scanning the driveway and she raises an eyebrow. "My brother, right?"

My cheeks redden.

"He, uhm... well he hasn't said anything to me today. I didn't expect him to be gone when we got back I guess."

She clicks her tongue and shakes her head. "So this is a thing now? You and Alec?"

How to even begin to answer that?

"Not officially, no. I think we like each other... but obviously it's more complicated than that."

She stops walking and turns to face me full on, her bullshit meter. "You *think* you like each other?"

I bite the inside of my cheek. "Okay, we know we like each other. That doesn't change how fucked up all this is." I look down at my phone again. "Or the fact that he has ghosted me all day."

Allie wraps her arm around me. "I'm sure he has a reason. I can't say I approve, but he'd be stupid to mess up with you. You're the complete opposite of anyone he's ever gone for, and I think that could be a good thing."

My stomach lurched a little bit. I'd only ever seen him with one other girl, Cass. It's obvious there were no similarities between us that much I was sure about.

"You don't approve?" I ask quietly.

She gives me a small smile, "Not really, Jo. No. Even if you weren't about to become my step sister, I don't want to see you get hurt. I don't know though, I haven't seen you together. Maybe things really are different with you, but until I know that I can't say that I'm on board with this. You understand, right?"

I nod. I do, I totally get it. She has zero reason to believe that this thing with her brother is going to end well. Hell, I have zero reason to believe it. I just have hope.

"Hey, want me to text him? I can come up with a reason?" Allie offers, but I shake my head.

"No, that's okay. If he wants me to know where he is he'll let me know."

She nods, and we begin walking back towards the house again.

"Good call. Want to watch a movie or something?" She asks.

"I think I'm going to take a bath. I want to wash this sunscreen off. Maybe later?"

Once I make it to my room and strip off my suit I force myself not to send another text. I set my phone on the floor next to the bathtub and turn up the volume, then click onto my bath time Spotify playlist. The water fills the tub and I slide into the steaming hot water.

How had I gone from hating him, to feeling sorry for him, to wanting him... and now to caring about him. Deeply. This roller-coaster of emotions was giving me whiplash.

The sound of my phone ringing jarred me from my thoughts and I jumped to it so quickly that water splashed everywhere.

Seeing Alec's name on the screen throws me for a loop.

He's calling me? I slide my finger to the right and press the phone to my ear.

Jo: Hello?

Alec: Shut up, I can't hear!

Wherever he is, it's loud. I can hear voices all around him, and the faint hum of music in the background.

Jo: Alec?

Alec: Yeah, I'm here. Sorry for the radio silence today, I came to talk shit out with Nate.

His was slurring pretty bad.

Alec: We're cool, but he invited people over and a party kind of sprung up. Hey, uh you think you can come get me? I don't think I should drive.

Jesus. I pull out the plug from the bath and let the water drain.

Jo: You definitely don't *sound* like you should drive. You don't want to stay there tonight?

I hear a whiny feminine voice on the other end.

Alec, why the hell are you trying to leave? You're supposed to be my partner this round.

Oh, hell no.

Jo: Send me the address, I'm on my way.

Alec: Really? You don't mind? I'm sorry if I'm fucking up your night.

I can't help but smile.

But then the voice is back and my smile disappears. This time the mystery girl is dialing up the heat. I can almost picture her attempting to drag him back into the party and away from his phone conversation with me.

Just hang up and come with me, you don't need to leave. Don't you want to-

I clear my throat abruptly, having no desire to let her finish that sentence.

Jo: No, it's fine. The address?

Alec: Yeah, I'm sending it now.

My phone beeps signaling that I've received the location.

Alec: Cass, please. I'm on the phone.

You have got to be kidding me.

The line goes dead and I don't think I've ever gotten dressed so fast in my life.

I want to be angry. How can I? He called *me*. If he wanted her he could have easily taken her, and I would have never known.

I repeat that sentiment to myself the entire way there.

I don't care that he didn't text me all day, and I don't care that he went to a party. All I care about is that when he did stop to think for a moment about how he wanted the night to play out, *he thought of me*.

CHAPTER TWENTY-ONE

You have reached your destination. My GPS exclaims as I pull up to Nate's house. There are dozens of cars parked along the street in front of the house. I pull out my phone and call Alec, hoping that he is expecting me and waiting.

No answer.

I shoot him a quick text letting him know I'm outside, but there comes no response.

Fuck.

I look down at my appearance and groan. I left in such a hurry, and the last thing I want to do is walk inside to find him. I'm wearing a pair of plaid Victoria's Secret pajama shorts and a white tank top. I did, thankfully, put on a bra before I left. However, my hair is piled on top of my head in a messy bun and all my makeup had already been washed off.

I try to call once more before biting the bullet and heading inside.

"Jo! What are you doing here?" I hear Kurt's friendly voice, and not long after I'm wrapped in a bear hug.

"Oh, hey! I'm here to pick up Alec, have you seen him?"

Kurt points towards the kitchen. "Last I saw he was playing beer pong in there."

I give him a smile and thank him.

On my way to the kitchen, I spot Nate leaning against the wall talking to a pretty brunette and our eyes meet. He gives me a cautious smile, and I return it. We haven't spoken since the incident, and I hope that we can move past it. Even if he was interested in more with me at one point in time, I still value the friendship that we were in the process of building.

In the kitchen, I find Alec at the beer pong table just as Kurt said. He's mid throw, and a scantily clad Cass is at his side. When the ball rang the cup she threw her arms around his waist and beamed up at him with congratulations.

My skin's on fire.

I storm over to him to announce myself.

"Alec." I say through gritted teeth.

His eyes light up when he sees me, "There she is!"

"Here I am." I reply, averting my gaze to Cass.

She looks me up and down. "Nice outfit, off to a slumber party?"

Yep. I hate her.

I manage a laugh just to spite her and try to think of a clever retort, but I have nothing. I'm seeing red, and I just want to get Alec and get out of here.

"You ready?" I ask him, and right as he begins to nod, Cass wraps her hand around his bicep.

"Uh no? What the hell. We're in the middle of a game."

That whiny voice was back. Did she really think that worked on guys? It was repulsive if you ask me.

"Oh shit, right. Do you mind if we finish up? Shouldn't be long, we're creaming them."

He *had* to be joking. The goofy grin on his face made it clear he had no clue I was seething.

I click my tongue. "Sure, I guess that's fine.".

Cass turns up her over-lined lips in a smirk as if to say she'd won, and I just roll my eyes. As much as I may want to put her in her place, she's not worth it.

I sit on a bar stool and watch as they make a swift victory over the two guys on the opposing team, or I should say as Alec made a swift victory. He carried the team. I think Cass made one cup the entire game.

Once they were finished, I hopped down and returned to meet him.

"Now are you ready?"

He smiles and nods, and I turn to head towards the door.

Once outside, I realized freaking Cass followed us. Please tell me she didn't think I was their taxi for the night? This bitch can call an Uber.

"Uh, what are you doing Cass?" I ask her, and she seems shocked that I'd addressed her.

"I need a ride, what does it look like?"

I clench my jaw tightly and shake my head, "Sorry, you'll have to find another ride."

Cass narrows her eyes and looks to Alec for back-up. "Seriously, Alec? What the hell is wrong with this girl?"

Alec looks at me with a sheepish grin, "She lives on the way, you don't mind right Jo?"

I couldn't even look to Cass. If I'd seen the victorious smirk she's sporting there's a good chance I'd strangle her. And him.

"Yeah, actually I do mind." I surprise myself with the admission, but I was standing by it.

"Aw, come on." He takes a step towards the passenger seat. "It's not a big deal. I can show you how to get there."

I can't believe this is happening. Sure he's drunk, but Jesus.

Cass moves to reach for the back door and slides into the Jeep without giving me a second look.

Still gritting my teeth together I get into the driver's seat and slam my door.

I listen to Alec's slurred directions and pull into Cass's driveway. The icing on the cake is her essentially begging him to come inside with her. He declined, but I'm so angry at this point it didn't even matter.

We drove the rest of the way home in silence. Well, I did. He made multiple attempts to talk to me, but I ignored each and every one of them. When I pull up to the house, I put the Jeep in park, removed the keys, and got out as quickly as possible. Stalking up to the house I leave him behind, not even swayed by the look of complete confusion on his drunken face.

I head straight for my bedroom knowing that he'll likely be right behind me.

"Jo, did I do something to upset you?" Alec's voice is low as he sticks his head in my doorway.

I let out a sarcastic laugh. "Oh, of course not. What could you have possibly done to upset me?"

He takes a few steps towards me and shrugs, "I have no fucking clue, but I'd appreciate it if you filled me in."

There's no way he's this clueless.

"I don't know, maybe you call and ask me to come get you and then make me wait while you let some girl hang all over you right in front of my face. Then to top it all off you make me give her a fucking ride home even after I said no. How cute is it that you know exactly how to get to her house, by the way? So *fucking* adorable."

Alec looks down at his feet, seemingly just now realizing that he screwed up.

"She was clearly surprised that you decided not to accompany her back inside for some late night fun, I hate that you had to turn her down on my account."

I didn't mean to get emotional. Hell, I didn't even know it until the tears were wetting my cheeks.

Alec is at my side in an instant, his thumbs wiping away the tears that he knows are his fault.

"Shit, I'm so sorry. I'm an idiot. I don't want Cass, you know that. I wasn't- I should have just left when you got there. I'm sorry."

I take a step away from him and shake my head. "No, it's whatever. I don't know why I'm crying. Just- I just want to go to sleep."

"Look, I said I'm sorry. I wasn't trying to hurt your feelings. I called because I wanted to be with you tonight, not anyone else."

I know he's telling the truth, but it doesn't make it hurt any less.

"I know that. I also know that seeing her throw herself at you hurt really fucking bad, Alec. And you not shutting it down hurt even worse. I guess I just- I thought we were-"

He cut me off, "Stop, okay? We are. She's nothing. You're right, and it won't happen again. I'm not used to this stuff. I'm shit at relationships and you know that, but you're right. I should have told her to take a hike, and next time I will."

He said relationship, and I want to tell my heart to calm down with the skipping.

We're still mad, heart. Okay?

"Jo? I'm sorry. Don't be mad at me."

He takes a step towards me and wraps his large hand around mine, rubbing circles over them with his thumb.

"Don't pull any shit like that again, okay? I'm not kidding. That was messed up."

He pulls me into him and lets out a sigh of relief.

"I won't, I promise. You're my girl, okay? I'll tell everyone tomorrow if you want. I'll tell Cass, and anyone else."

I shake my head. "You're drunk. Tomorrow that will be the last thing you want to do."

He silences me with a kiss. It's a sweet one, one full of promise and intention.

"I think you're wrong. I think even when I'm completely sober I'll want everyone to know your mine."

If only life were so simple.

CHAPTER TWENTY-TWO

The next morning, neither one of us mentioned Alec's sudden urge to out our feelings for each other to the world, and for now I'm okay with that. With the wedding so close it seems like an irresponsible and selfish decision to make.

It's becoming harder and harder to keep these feelings locked up behind closed doors. I crave him every moment of every day, and when it finally came time to get my hands on him... it was *everything*. We were addicts clawing, ravenous just to get one more fix.

Every night when I tiptoe down those stairs into his bedroom it's like a rush, and once I fall into his bed, it's like I could finally breathe.

Sometimes it was rough and hard, and others it was slow and gentle... but every single time it was pure passion. When our bodies fuse together it's electric, like there are thousands of tiny sparks constantly igniting on our skin- lighting up the world around us, but only we could see it.

"Only a few more days until the wedding," I say to him as we lie on his bed. "Then we have an entire week together while our parents on their honeymoon."

He exhales and pulls me in tighter. "You know what I'm most looking forward to?"

"What?"

His deep voice right next to my ear gives me chills. "Spending the night with you. You in my bed when I go to sleep, and then getting to wake up next to you."

My inner Goddess is reveling in this admission. "That sounds nice."

I roll over so that our eyes meet and I can't help but smile. How did we get here? It feels like yesterday this beautiful man was the last person on the planet I wanted to be stuck in the same room with, but now I'd do anything to be by his side.

"Just nice?" His words taunt me.

I roll my eyes and let out a giggle, "Okay, more than nice."

His hands began to roam my body. First my face, then down my neck. He traces my collarbones and then down the curves of my breasts. My breath catches and a small moan escapes my lips.

"How is your skin so soft?" He whispers into my neck.

My legs part for him out of pure instinct, and the devilish grin on his face lets me know that is exactly what he wants. His hand continues to slide down my body until his palm cups the place that needs him the most. A single finger slips inside my crease, while his thumb slides back and forth over the bundle of nerves sending me into the abyss.

"Always so ready for me," he murmurs quietly.

"Y-yes," I manage to choke out. "Always."

His dark hair is disheveled, and his green eyes seem to be endless right now. The ink on his body tightens and contorts with every movement of his hard body as he pleasures me with his fingers. It shouldn't be legal for a man to be this fucking sexy. I think it's the wild nature of our encounters that really gets me going. The pure primal lust, the dangerously taboo aura that envelopes us... it's intoxicating.

"Perfect." Alec groaned, "Absolutely perfect." His eyes rake over my body before his lips crash into mine possessively. Our bodies know exactly what the other is wanting now, and his fingers work magic inside me.

As he takes control of my body I realize something. Something that makes the climbing climax so much more intense- I'm completely and utterly his. I'm falling hard and fast... and it terrifies me. The crash of clarity washes over me like a tidal wave simultaneously with the orgasm. Every inch of my body shudders around him and I fight to catch my breath.

"You know what else I can't wait for?" Alec rasps, pulling my body to where it fits perfectly against his.

"What's that?" I say softly.

He looks down at me with a need so strong it causes me to tense. "Making you scream my name. Getting to take you without holding back, and not giving a fuck who hears it."

Oh.

I bite my lower lip as desire creeps up my spine. "Allie will still be here, we won't be completely alone."

"Let me handle that." He says before kissing me again. "Now, you need to get out of here before the sun comes up."

I glance over at his phone on the nightstand and press the home button. It's almost four AM.

Letting out a groan, I roll off the bed. Instead of putting my own clothes back on I grab his black t-shirt from the floor and pull it over my head. It smells like him. I snag a pair of his briefs too.

"I like you in my clothes." He says, placing his arms behind his head and admiring me.

"You aren't getting them back either." I reply, flashing him a flirty smile before making my way up the stairs and back towards my room.

"It's less than twenty-four hours before I walk down the aisle, can you believe that?" My mother exclaims as she twirls around the bedroom like a school girl. I've never seen her look so genuinely happy. Sean's out with his business associates for celebratory drinks, but mom wants to stay in tonight. She's a tightly wound bundle of nervous energy.

"It's going to be perfect." I say, placing a kiss on her cheek.

"You've hung up your dress, right? And laid everything out? Your shoes? What about-"

"Mom," I interrupt her spiral. "Come down off the ledge a little, everything is going to be fine."

She gives me a reassuring smile, "You're right honey, I'm sorry. I'm just so nervous."

"Of course you are, but don't be. Just relax, we have everything covered."

As I shut the door behind me and retreat into my own room, I replay the events of the summer so far in my mind. It's truly been a whirlwind, and tomorrow will be no different.

The rehearsal dinner went well tonight, even though the best man had failed to show up. No one looked surprised when Alec was nowhere to be found, well except for me. I'd been disappointed, though I tried to mask it.

The surprise came when Sean mentioned that since Alec is the best man, that he's going to be the one to escort me down the aisle. I know my cheeks must have reddened because he gave my shoulder a reassuring squeeze.

"Look, he will show up. He may try to fight this up until the final hour, but I know my son would never miss my wedding." I try to muster a smile, even though it's forced. "In the event that he doesn't, you'll just walk with my business partner Bill. He's escorting Allie, but I know he'd be happy to have both of you on his arms. Either way, it'll work out."

Sean thought my rosy cheeks were because I worried I'd end up walking alone, when in reality it was because the thought of doing something so intimate... so romantic with Alec made my heart feel like it was beating out of my chest. We'd be touching in front of everyone, arms linked and walking side by side. We'd be surrounded by literal hearts and flowers.

"I'm not worried, it will be fine. I'm sure he will show up." I say to Sean, and he places a quick peck on my cheek.

Now, as I lay in my bed, I fight the urge to walk downstairs to Alec's empty bed. Instead, I take out my phone and type a quick message out to him.

Jo: Missed you tonight at the rehearsal. You're supposed to escort me tomorrow, don't leave me hanging.

It takes a few moments before I get a response.

Alec: I didn't think walking in a straight line required too much rehearsing.

A smile creeps onto my lips.

Jo: True, it's hard to mess up unless you have one too many shots before the big moment.

Alec: Now that I can't promise. I'm going to need a little help getting through the whole circus act.

I roll my eyes.

Jo: You'll have me.

Alec: I'll be there.

That was enough, for now.

Jo: Good. See you tomorrow.

Alec: Sweet dreams, baby.

When he called me r that it never ceased to make my heart skip a beat. Full of happiness, satisfaction, and *hope*- I drift off to sleep.

CHAPTER TWENTY-THREE

So far today I had learned two things about weddings; One, they are stressful as hell. I have been running around like a chicken with my head cut off for the last four hours trying to make sure everything is in order. Two, everyone cries. Like constantly. The bridesmaids cried when they saw my mother in her wedding gown, and they cried again when she read aloud the letter Sean had written. My grandmother cried when she saw everyone else cry, and my emotionally stunted ass tried to stay as far away from the tears as possible.

When I found a moment to escape from the room, it was slowly beginning to feel like it was losing air supply, I took the chance without a second thought. Bracing myself against a column outside I took a few deep breaths and tried to center myself.

"Jesus Christ, why is everyone so fucking emotional." I say under my breath.

"It's a wedding, it's kind of meant to be a heartwarming occasion."

The sound of Nate's voice surprises me, and I jump.

"Sorry, didn't mean to scare you. I was walking by and wanted to make sure you were okay."

"No- No, I'm fine. Thank you, I just needed to catch my breath. What are you doing here?" I ask.

"I told you that Alec and I had been friends since diapers. My dad and Sean have been friends since college, he's in the wedding too." Nate explains, and I nod.

"Oh," the awkward tension filling the air. This is the first time we'd spoken since the fight between him and Alec.

"Look," We both said at the same time, followed by laughter. Thank God for that, the tension seemed to ease a bit.

"I'll go first, I'm sorry about what happened that night. I'd had a good bit to drink and I didn't mean to make you uncomfortable. I also had no clue that the vibes coming off Alec had nothing to do with hating you, I should have seen it sooner."

I still.

"He- he told you?" I stammer.

"No, he didn't have to. We've come to blows twice in all the years we've known each other. The first time was right after he lost his mom, and he just needed someone to take it out on. The second was over you. As soon as I saw the way he reacted when I touched you, I should have known. He's very possessive over you, very protective. I knew when he lunged at me that you were important, that he gave a shit no matter how hard he was trying to hide it."

I considered his words, still not speaking. What could I possibly say?

"No one else suspects anything, at least not that I know of." He says, in a reassuring tone. "I do have to ask though, what do you see coming out of this? I care about you, Jo. I really do. I get that you may not feel the same way, and I'll respect that. Just- just be careful okay?" His eyes are full of sincerity as he speaks.

"I care about you too, Nate. You have become someone I really depend on, and I don't want to lose that. I don't have many real friends, and I want to keep you in my life. I didn't mean for this to happen with Alec, honestly. As cliche as it sounds, it just did. I have no clue what is going to come out of it, but at this point I'll never forgive myself if I don't see it through."

He nods and wraps an arm around me. "Fair enough. Like I said, I'll respect it. I'm here though, okay? If shit turns bad, just call me."

"Thanks, Nate. I will." I hug him back, and let him hold me a little longer. It's nice to have yet another friend know the truth, and even more so that it's someone I'd been so scared of losing.

"I need to get back in there, it's almost showtime." I say to him as I break away from the embrace.

"Alright, and Jo?" He calls out.

"Yes?"

"You look beautiful."

And then he turns and heads back towards the cabin where the groomsmen are preparing.

I look down at the blush pink silk gown that hugs my curves like it's been created specifically for my body. I really do love this dress, and the compliment from Nate has given me a confidence boost that I needed going into today.

I take in one last deep breath before pushing my way back into the bridal room.

"There you are!" my mother exclaims, rushing to my side.

"Sorry, I needed some air." I say, apologetically.

She wraps her arms around me and spoke softly, so that only I could hear her. "I know there is a lot going on, honey. Thank you for everything. Today wouldn't have been possible without you." She presses her lips to my cheek and then giggles as she tries to smudge off the imprint from her red lipstick.

"You are a beautiful bride, Mom. Really, you look incredible."

Tears prick at the corners of her eyes, and causes a lump to form in the back of my throat.

"God, please don't cry again. The makeup artist is going to kill us."

We both laugh and hug for a few more seconds.

The photographer sticks her head in the doorway to tell us it's time to line up.

"Are you ready?" I ask her.

"Yes. So very ready." She answers.

The sound of Canon in D played by a string quartet fills my ears. I stand on my mark and wait for the signal to start walking. I feel him at my side and slide my arm into his.

"You made it." I whisper, not even trying to hide the smile on my face.

"I said I would, didn't I?" He replies.

I want to lean into him. I want to make it clear that he was mine, but I couldn't. Instead, I'd just have to play pretend. I imagine that everything is different. I imagine that he's my date, and that every time someone stops to tell us what a beautiful couple we make, that he'd squeeze my hand proudly.

"Ready?" he asks as the doors began to open slowly and the music approaches our queue.

"Let's do it." I respond.

We walk down the aisle covered in flower petals and when we reach the end he releases me. We take our places on each side of where our parents will soon stand.

Throughout the ceremony our gazes continued to connect. We'd lock onto one another, and at times I worried that someone may notice. The energy buzzes between us. It seems impossible that we were the only two people here that could sense it.

When it came time for them to read the vows they'd written, the mood shifts.

Sean spoke first.

"Kathleen, I marry you with my eyes wide open. You have helped me let go of the past, and I embrace the future. Thank you for making me laugh again. I offer myself to you as a partner in life. I vow to love you in sickness and in health. I commit myself to encourage you in good times and in bad. I will cherish and respect you all the days of our life together. Starting anew once again, I give thanks that I have found you. May our marriage be a gift to the world and our families, as your love is a gift to me. God has given us a second chance at happiness, and I intend to make every second count."

Damn, Sean. The beautiful words spoken took me by surprise, as did the tears now beginning to stream down my face. This man did truly love my mother. I looked to Alec, but when he locked his gaze with mine there was something new behind his eyes. I furrowed my brow in confusion, but he looked away.

Next, my mother began to read out her vows.

"Sean, since I have found you, I have found a new life. The decision to commit to share that life with you is one I make happily and with full confidence in our love. Because of you, I laugh, I smile and I dare to dream again. I look forward with great joy to spending the rest of my life with you, caring for you, nurturing you, being there for you in all that life has in store for us, and I vow to be true and faithful for as long as we both shall live. I come today to give you my love, to give you my heart and my hope for our future together. I promise to bring you joy, and to learn to love you more each day, through all the days of our lives."

There isn't a dry eye in the place, well- not counting Alec. He looks pained, and he refuses to meet my gaze.

The rest of the ceremony is a blur. All I can think about is getting to him and finding out what's wrong. His mood shifted so quickly, and it hurts to see him upset.

After the minister announced them as husband and wife, it's time to walk out together. With our arms linked, we walk out in silence.. Once out the large double doors he releases me and walks away, leaving me standing there alone.

"Alec?" I call after him, but he ignores me disappearing into the men's restroom.

CHAPTER TWENTY-FOUR

He misses the reception. He misses the first dance, and he misses the cutting of the cake. I find myself staring at the doors waiting for him to walk into the ballroom and apologize for bailing, but he doesn't. I want to go look for him, but I can't. I can't leave my mother, not on her wedding day.

When it comes time to give my speech as Maid of Honor, I take the microphone and try to rally my spirits, but it's hard. There's so many emotions swirling inside my head, but mainly it's confusion.

"When you told me that you had met someone new, and that he'd asked you to marry him there were many thoughts and emotions running through my mind. I had no clue what to expect, and most of all I was terrified of watching you get hurt again. Losing Dad was excruciating, but even worse was watching my strong and fearless mother suffer. Seeing you in so much pain was the hardest thing I've ever had to experience, and I would rather walk through fire than to ever see you hurt that way again. This whole thing scared the crap out of me to put it candidly. But, then I saw you with Sean. You have found someone who treats you with love and respect; who is a *real* partner; and who treats you like the incredible woman you are. I am so happy for you and Sean, and wish you both nothing but happiness as you get this second chance at a lifetime of love."

I raise my glass of champagne in the air, "Cheers to the happy couple."

The room erupts in cheers and glasses clinking together, and the newly married Mr. and Mrs. Sean Miller both embrace me lovingly.

"Thank you, Josephine. That was beautiful." Sean says.

Just then I notice the venue host look to Sean and gesture to the microphone. Sean shakes his head as if to tell him to move on. It hits me that the host is wondering about the Best Man's speech, and my heart breaks.

Allie's gaze catches mine and I can see that she is disappointed in her brother.

"He left didn't he?" I ask her quietly.

"I don't know, probably. I don't know why I'm surprised, it's to be expected." She replies.

"No, it isn't. It wouldn't have killed him to just- to just fucking be here."

Her eyes widen. "You okay?"

"No. He should have stayed, he should have been here for his family." Tears prick at my eyes again. "Dammit, I don't want to cry anymore today."

"You mean he should have been here for you?" She whispered, taking my hand in hers. "We all knew he wasn't exactly thrilled about the wedding, but you thought he'd do it for you. I won't lie, I kind of thought so too."

She's right. I knew he didn't give a shit about this whole *circus* as he'd called it, but I did think he'd deal with it for me. I thought he'd want to spend time with me, not bail as soon as his duty was finished.

I fought the urge to pull out my phone and text him, instead taking Allie's outstretched arms and heading to the dance floor.

It didn't take long before Nate asked if he could cut in, and I let him.

"Looks like Alec bolted." He says when I press my head against his chest.

"Yep, looks like it." I respond, coldly.

"Don't be too hard on him, Jo. This wasn't easy for him. You know that."

I look up at Nate and narrow my eyes.

"Look, I'm not saying him leaving is okay. I'm just saying-"

"Don't defend him on this one, okay? Just don't." I interject, and he simply nods. "Let's just dance, no more talking. Please?"

Instead of responding, Nate tightens his grip on me and we dance to an instrumental version of some Elvis song.

A few hours pass before it's time for the big send off. Two rows of guests form on either side of the walkway and toss hand-fulls of birdseed over the heads of the bride and groom. They are ushered into a white stretch limo and without another word are off to the airport. This time tomorrow they will be lounging on a sandy beach off a remote island.

I take Nate up on his offer for a ride home, and when we pull up, I exit the car and thank him. He doesn't ask to come in, instead silently pulls away. I think he knows I'm emotionally exhausted. I walk in on the tail end of a conversation between Allie and Alec.

"You're an idiot, you know that right." I hear her say to him.

I still, trying to silence my breathing so they don't realize I've come home.

"Al, it's not that big of a deal. I doubt anyone even noticed I left."

I hear her scoff, "She did. You know she did. You should have seen her face."

"I don't know what you're talking about." He deadpans.

My stomach lurches.

"Yeah, okay. I guess you think I'm an idiot. I see what's happening between you and Jo. I don't know what you are trying to get out of this, but she cares about you. Like she *really* cares about you. Is it just another game? Are you just trying to screw with her?"

Silence.

I imagine that his mind is reeling over the realization that his little sister knows about us.

"Nothing? You're just going to ignore me too?" She prods.

"There is nothing going on with Jo."

His voice is so flat, so callous. A wave of nausea hits me.

"I knew you could be cold, but to deny something so obvious is just- well it's really disappointing Alec." Allie's voice is direct.

"Drop it, Al."

"And what about her? Will she drop it?" She asks.

"I don't give a shit, there is nothing-"

I can't listen to anymore, so I do the only thing I can think of that will stop the conversation.

"Don't worry about me, I'll drop it. I mean, it's not like there was anything going on in the first place. Right, Alec?"

His face goes white.

Good.

"Jo, I-" Alec begins, but I hold up a hand.

"Don't bother." I convey my disgust with my eyes, and I can tell by the shudder that he got the message loud and clear.

I turn on my heels and take the stairs two at a time, needing to put as much distance between us as possible. I turn the lock and slide down the closed door, pressing all my weight against it. The tears are falling, and I hear him approach the door.

"Please, I didn't mean that and you know it." His voice is quiet.

"Just go away, I can't do this tonight." I say through the sobs.

"Jo, please." The pleading in his voice makes it hard to stand my ground.

But I do.

"No. Not tonight. You need to go."

There is silence for a while, but then I hear his footsteps leading away from the door and down the stairs. A few seconds later there is a loud slam from his bedroom door.

I can't explain why I am so upset, but my heart is being ripped to shreds.

I riffle through the small clutch resting on my bed for my phone.

My fingers quickly type in Drake's number and I try to hold back the tears as it rings.

Please pick up.

"JoJo?" His sleepy voice calls out.

I lose all composure and sob into the phone.

"Jesus, what's wrong?" He sounds more alert now.

I take a deep breath, trying to calm myself so I can speak.

"I'm an idiot. That's what is wrong."

I can hear him shift in the bed.

"What did he do?"

It should be a sign that he knew exactly what I was upset about.

"For one, he left me at the wedding. He just fucking bolted. That isn't even the worst part. I walked in on him making it very clear that I mean absolutely nothing to him. How could I be so stupid?"

It's a wonder that he can understand anything I am saying through the tears.

"JoJo, you aren't stupid. If anything, he's the idiot here, not you."

"I'm sorry I woke you, I just- I just need my best friend." My words come out in almost a whisper. "Could we maybe do that thing where we stay on the phone until I fall asleep?"

We hadn't done that in years. After my father died there were many nights that I couldn't sleep because if I did, the nightmares would come. They forced me to relive that day over and over. Drake would stay on the phone with me, not saying a word. I don't know why, but it helped. It helped to know that someone was there with me.

"Of course." He coos.

I lie down with the phone against my ear and bury myself in the blankets. I try not to think of Alec, but it's impossible.

He never promised me anything, and we'd never exclusively defined what was happening between us. He'd never guaranteed that he'd stay at the wedding once his role had been completed.

That didn't change the fact that I'd hoped he would stay. That he'd ask me to dance like Nate had, or that he would give his father the gift of actually saying a few words in support of his happiness.

If it had just been that I may have been okay. I figured all the intimacy of the ceremony spooked him. I knew that was probably why he bolted.

What hurt the worst was that he'd lied when he said he would gladly tell anyone that I was his girl. That night when he'd drunkenly claimed that he was proud of it... that he would tell everyone if that's what I wanted. Tonight proved that those claims were nothing but a load of shit. He'd been presented with the perfect opportunity to admit his feelings for me, but instead he'd insisted that I meant nothing. That *we* were nothing.

In this moment I couldn't even gauge my own feelings anymore. Had any of this been real? Were these feelings genuine? Or had we just been sucked into some whirlwind fling because it was forbidden? We all want what we aren't supposed to have, but was that all this was?

CHAPTER TWENTY-FIVE

I wake up this morning to the sound of light knocking on my bedroom door.
"Jo? It's Allie. Can I come in?"
I roll out from under my comforter and walk to the door.
When I open it she stands there with a sweet smile.
"I made breakfast, come eat with me?"
How could I refuse that? Not that I wanted to. I didn't actually eat much yesterday, and my stomach started growling the moment she mentioned food.
Downstairs, I plopped into one of the chairs at the kitchen table and took in the spread. She'd made pancakes, though I couldn't tell if they were blueberry or chocolate chip.
"This looks great." I cut into the stack of pancakes and shovel a bite into my mouth.
Blueberry.
"And they taste incredible. Thanks, Allie." I give her an appreciative smile, and she beams.
Alec must've heard my voice because he enters the room and takes a seat next to me.
"Can we talk?" He asks.

I completely avoid eye contact, "I'm eating."

Allie puts a plate of pancakes in front of her brother and lets out an exasperated breath.

"Thanks." He grits out.

"Sure. You know, you missed a pretty great reception last night. Dad and Kathleen had a blast." I raise an eyebrow at Allie, wondering why she's bringing this up again.

Alec nods, but didn't respond.

She continues, "The DJ was really good. He actually played some current music every so often, stuff we could actually dance to. Right Jo?"

Where was she going with this?

I shrug my shoulders and take another bite.

"I mean, our dance was interrupted when Nate cut in... but I was fine with it. He's such a gentlemen, you know?" The look Allie was giving Alec was intense, like she was daring him to respond.

His eyes are on me, burning through me.

Allie shows no sign of backing down. "In fact, he gave you a ride home didn't he Jo? I mean, I'm sure you were planning on riding back with my brother- but we all know how that turned out."

Shit. She was baiting him, looking for a reaction.

"What the fuck, Jo?" He growls out.

Excuse me? That's it, I broke.

"I'm sorry, but who the hell do you think you are?" I ask him through gritted teeth. "Do you actually think you get to be angry here? Do you seriously feel like you have a leg to stand on? How *dare* you."

I push away the plate of uneaten pancakes and stand. "Yes, we danced together because you fucking disappeared and left me alone. He drove me home because it was either that or call an Uber because I had *planned* on coming home with you."

His eyes shifted. Regret? Maybe, but right now I don't care.

"Oh, and by the way-" I pointed to Allie, "She knew. She knew the truth when you tried to lie about it last night. She figured it out weeks ago. And Nate? He knows too. So does V."

I take a step towards him. "It's obvious to them, and when they confronted me about it I didn't hide it. Not like you did last night. What was it you said? There was *nothing* between us? Good to know."

"Can we please talk in private?" He asks, but I shake my head.

"No, I don't want to. Not yet. Hearing that last night hurt. It hurt really fucking bad."

He stands and closes the space between us, placing his hands on my cheeks. "I'm sorry, okay? I messed up. I'm sorry."

The tears threatening to fall, but I blink them back.

"Hearing my dad say that stuff to your mom... I just- it brought back memories. I don't like hearing him talk that way about another woman. And then you just looked so happy. When they were talking about love... and commitment. I could see it in your eyes. That's not me. I got freaked out, Jo. I'm sorry."

I try to wriggle out of his grasp but he tightens his hold.

"I shouldn't have bolted, and I damn sure shouldn't have left you with fucking Nate to look after you."

"Is that what this is about? You're jealous of-"

He cut me off. "No, of course not. I'm pissed at myself for giving him that opening. It should have been me there with you." His grasp on my face loosened, and I looked away.

When my eyes meet with Allie's she was looking back and forth between us, and I can see the confusion. This is the first time she'd seen him interact with me like this.

"Look at me." He said softly.

I couldn't. If I looked at him now I wouldn't be able to hold back the tears.

"Jo, look at me. I fucked up."

Keeping my head turned away I whisper, "You said we were nothing."

"I lied. You know it was a lie. This-" he pressed his forehead to mine, "This isn't nothing."

Dammit. There go the tears.

He looks at Allie, "You hear that? I lied. I care about her. It's not nothing."

He turned his attention back to me. "You could never be nothing, not to me." He pressed his lips to my temple and my final wall of defense fell away. I let my arms wrap around his waist and I could his body relaxed a little. He actually let out a sigh of relief.

"What the hell is going on?" A deep voice boomed and we instinctively ripped apart from one another.

What I saw in front of me made me want to vomit.

Sean and my mother stared at us with a mixture of confusion and anger.

No-one spoke.

My mother's hand was placed over her mouth but it didn't hide her shocked expression.

"Is everyone suddenly mute? I asked, what the hell is going on?" Sean growls.

Allie breaks the silence as she stammered, "Wh- what are you doing here?"

"Passports. We forgot the passports." My mother says, barely above a whisper.

"Allie, upstairs. Now."

It was evident Allie had never heard her father speak that way by the fear in her eyes.

"Daddy, don't-" She attempts to calm him, but he shuts her down.

"Now."

The command was clear, and she obeyed.

Sean takes a step forward and Alec moves in front of me protectively.

"How could you do this, son? Do you hate me this much? Was it so hard for you to just let me be happy?" The accusation in his tone was harsh. He was insinuating exactly what Allie thought at first, and what I had feared the most. He thought Alec had done this to get back at his father.

"This has nothing to do with you." Alec said plainly.

"How can you expect me to believe that?" Sean countered.

"I don't care what you believe." He spit out.

My mother advanced toward me but Alec didn't budge. "Honey, you aren't- you aren't having a relationship with him are you?"

Her tone was even, but I knew she was barely holding it together.

"Of course they are, look at them!" Sean yelled. "Why was she crying? What were you apologizing for? Did he hurt you Josephine?"

All of the air had been pulled from the room and I couldn't breathe.

"N-No." I managed.

"Did you really just ask if I fucking hurt her?" Alec boomed.

This is getting out of hand, quickly.

My mother wraps her hand around my wrist and begins to gently pull me towards the door.

"Let's give them some space, I think they need to talk."

This is the last thing I want to do. I can't leave Alec to deal with Sean's anger alone.

Alec seems to agree with her though. "Jo, go with her. It's fine."

I shake my head, "No, I need to stay-"

His eyes plead with me to listen. "Please, let me handle this."

I allowed my mother to lead me into the living room and towards the door. Their shouts begin to sound muffled the farther we got from the kitchen. I hear fragments of what's being said and my heart is slowly breaking.

"Took advantage of."

"A child."

"Ruined everything."

"Fucking disappointment."

I try to turn around, but my mother pulls me out the door.

"He didn't take advantage of me, I have to tell Sean the truth. Please mom."

My mother had tears in her eyes. "How could you do this, Josephine? He's your step brother. We're supposed to be a family. This is- This is wrong."

"No, we met before. I had no clue who he was. I didn't know, I swear. We tried to stop it, to end things but we couldn't." I try to explain everything to her, but she just continues to shake her head in disbelief.

The sound of a slamming door takes my attention away from my mother, and the sound of tires peeling out of the driveway causes me to dart back inside.

Sean's face is buried in his hands as he sits at the bar.

"Where did he go?" I ask, but Sean doesn't look up.

"Sean?" My mother's quiet voice got through to him.

"He left, and I doubt he's coming back." His gaze met mine, "I don't know what to say, Josephine. I don't understand how this happened."

"You have to call him, you have to tell him to come home. We can figure this out." I plead with him.

"I think its best he stay away for a while." Sean says in a low, flat voice. "Kathleen, I imagine you'll understand the need to delay our flight."

"Of course." My mother replies as she goes to her husband's side and caresses his back.

What just happened? How had everything gone from zero to one hundred in sixty seconds? My lungs constrict and my heart is pounding. Where do we go from here?

CHAPTER TWENTY-SIX

Two days. Forty-eight hours. Two thousand eight hundred and eighty minutes.

That's how long it had been since everything blew up around me.

I'd refused to leave my bedroom. I felt like a ghost, a shell of myself just floating around waiting for the next explosion. I couldn't face my mother or Sean. Their eyes were filled with things that I wasn't used to, disappointment.

I could hear them arguing every so often. Sean would yell and my mother would cry. The blame was so clearly being thrust on Alec. They viewed me as the victim in some sick game, that I had been so easily manipulated by the bad boy. With every word said against him my patience wore thinner. The whirlpool of emotions swirling within me was bubbling to the surface, and it wouldn't stay contained much longer.

His phone hadn't turned on once since he left. I know this because I'd called it a hundred times. It never rang, only sending me straight to voicemail.

"Please just call me, we need to figure this out." I would plead into the phone.

I could understand their reaction initially, but fuck at some point this had to stop. I am not a child for God's sake. We're consenting adults, and even though the circumstances surrounding our relationship are shit... it doesn't change *anything*.

Allie crawls into my bed and settles underneath the comforter with me.

"Hey." She says quietly.

"Hey."

She must've seen the question forming on the tip of my tongue. "I haven't heard from him."

I grit my teeth and nod.

"They can't be angry forever. This will blow over, and we can-"

I stop her. "We can what? Go back to normal? What the hell is normal about this?"

She says nothing. I should feel bad about snapping at her, but instead I'm numb.

"I need to talk to them. I need for them to understand that this isn't what they think it is. Hell, it may have started as something dirty and wrong... but not anymore. It's real."

Allie pulls me into her, "I just don't think you should be the only one fighting this battle, Jo. I don't understand why he left. How could he leave you here to deal with this on your own?"

I considered this for a moment, but only for a moment.

"The night we first talked about where this was going, about what we wanted- he was holding back. I could feel that he cared for me, but he fought it so hard. Do you know why?"

She shook her head.

"He was scared of disappointing me. He thinks he's broken. Damaged goods. He truly believes that he doesn't deserve to have someone care for him the way that I do. He was so sure that in the end he would end up disappointing me and that I would hate him. He said if I ever hated him it would finish off whatever was left of his ability to care."

Allie looks pained.

"I heard your dad tell him he was a *fucking disappointment* before my Mother pulled me outside. It must have triggered something inside him. After everything he's done, after everything he's been through-"

My face begins to heat up and a lump forms at the back of my throat.

"You really care about him don't you?" She asks in a hushed tone.

"You're damn right I do."

"He's lucky to have someone like you in his corner. You seem to only see the good." The look of realization and acceptance flashes on her face.

"I see the dark, I just know that there is more to him than his demons. You don't go through what he did without getting a little fucked up. He stepped up when your father stepped back, Allie."

The tears streaming down Allie's cheeks mirror my own.

"In fact, I think I'll tell him that myself."

There's a newfound strength radiating inside me, and I need to act on it before I lose my nerve.

I find them in the den, seated next to one another on the sofa watching 20/20.

"I need to talk, and I need you to listen. Both of you."

"Josephine-" My mother begins, but I shake my head.

"Please, just listen. Hear me out, and then I'll do the same."

They both nod in reluctant agreement.

"My first night here I went to Shooter's, there I met a guy who I instantly connected with. Imagine my surprise when I discovered this guy was your son." I maintained eye contact with Sean as I spoke.

"What began as an undeniable spark became animosity. Alec was so against the idea of my mother and I being here, and he made it pretty fucking hard to think of him as a decent human being. Slowly, ever so slowly... I was able to chip away at those walls bit by bit. And that spark from the first night? It never went away. We tried to fight it. Why would we want this?"

Shocked they were still remaining silent, I continued.

"Why would any two people *want* to end up in this situation? I sure as hell never wanted this. To burn so intensely for someone and be forced to stay quiet about it is nothing other than pure punishment."

The sadness is gone. It'd been replaced with anger, and a need to defend the person I cared about.

"He's broken, you know? He tries to hide it with the tattoos and give no fucks attitude, but it's an act. What happened with his mother shattered him."

Sean looks as if I'd slapped him. "And you think her death didn't affect me or Allie? You don't see us acting out! I lost my wife, Josephine. The mother of my children."

There's no way he was this clueless. There's no way he didn't see what he'd put his son through.

"I get that, I do. You need to understand something, but you aren't going to like it." I take a deep breath.

"Where were you?" I ask.

"Excuse me?" He responds, clearly agitated.

"When she was dying, where were you? I know where Alec was, but where were you?"

His jaw clenches.

"You weren't here. You threw yourself into work because you couldn't stand to watch what was happening to the woman you loved. I can't begin to imply that I know what that must have been like, but I can imagine it was excruciating. We all handle grief differently, and in this case you chose to distance yourself from it. But Alec? He didn't get that choice. Allie was here alone with her dying mother during some of the most trying times in a young girl's life. Her only other parent was basically MIA, so he dropped everything and moved back home. He became his mother's caregiver. In the end, she looked to him for support. You had your reasons, but the hard truth to swallow is you abandoned your family when they needed you."

More silence.

"He isn't perfect, in fact he's far from it. But what he is- is a boy who stepped up when you couldn't. He feels like he wasn't enough to save her though. It created a complex within him that he now battles daily. He watched her wait for her husband to come home, and he watched her wither away. It shouldn't have been Alec that sat by her death bed. It shouldn't have been him who had to move home to take care of his little sister because her mother was bed ridden and her father couldn't handle it. He did it for his family, only to be called a *fucking disappointment* by the one person who let him down the most."

I watch Sean's eyes and see the exact moment when his anger fades to heartbreak. My mother's gaze is averted, undoubtedly trying to keep from sobbing.

"I- I made so many mistakes." Sean whispers. "I didn't realize-"

He stands from the sofa and begins to pace. "I couldn't bear to see her like that. Don't you think I regret it every single day? That I wasn't there for her? That I wasn't there for them?"

"Have you ever told him that?" I ask plainly.

The look on his face says no.

There's another long stretch of silence.

"I promised I would hear you out if you let me speak, so I will." I offer.

"I think that's enough for one evening." My mother says quietly.

I nod and begin to walk back towards the stairs.

"Josephine," Sean calls out, and I stop. "I need you to know I don't think of him that way. I love my son, he could never be a disappointment."

I appreciate the sentiment, but it's time for action. No more empty words.

"He needs to hear that, not me." I turn and make my way up to my room.

Relief. A huge weight has been lifted off my shoulders.

Whatever happens next, at least I know I'd done everything I could. The ball is in their court now, but I can't help but feel hopeful that this could be the first step towards healing for Alec and his father.

CHAPTER TWENTY-SEVEN

I tried not to let the excitement of knowing he would be under the same roof as me at any moment completely overwhelm me. He's finally coming home to talk to his father, a conversation that's bound to be more emotionally charged than either man is prepared for. I found myself hoping that my outburst would spark something in Sean, and that he would finally give his son the apology he deserved.

I also hoped that Alec would hear him out, and that the two could have a productive talk where both sides got to get everything off their chest.

It's been almost a week since I've seen him, and if anyone gets near me the pounding in my chest will give away just how close I am to losing all the composure I'd managed to muster.

"Josephine," my mother says in a soft voice, placing her palm against my back. "I think we should get out of the house for a few hours, let them talk alone without any distractions."

Not fucking happening.

"I'm not going anywhere." I say, standing firm in my position by the front door.

She sighs, but doesn't push me. She likely knew before even suggesting it that I wouldn't budge.

When Alec's car pulls into the driveway, my heart tightens in my chest.

He's wearing those black skinny jeans that I love so much, the ones with the rips at the knees. The solid black T-shirt completes his bleak ensemble, and the solemn expression on his face makes it look more like he's about to walk into a funeral home than the place he's lived for all these years.

Our eyes meet, and I try to manage a small smile. He doesn't return it, instead furrows his brows and bites his lip.

"I've missed you." I say to him in the softest voice I can once I know for sure no one else can hear me.

"Me too." He says. "Sorry for being MIA. Everything just got so fucked up and I needed to figure out what to do next."

I want to tell him how pissed I am that he left me here to deal with this mess alone, but I don't. Instead, I shrug and lace my fingers through his.

"I know why you had to go, it's okay." The forgiveness in my words seems to relax him a bit, which in turn relaxes me.

He gives my hand a light squeeze, and the reassurance I feel from the small gesture is monumental.

"Are you ready for this?" I ask.

"Nope, but what choice do I have?" He replies quickly. "Anyways, I'll find you afterwards so we can talk. I want to get this shit over with."

The sudden loss of his touch as he releases my hand makes me ache, but I know he needs to do this. I watch as he disappears into his father's study and closes the door behind him.

It's quiet in there, too quiet. I fully expected to hear screaming, maybe even the sound of a decorative vase being thrown at the wall.

Okay, maybe that's a bit dramatic, but even still... it seems much too calm. It reminds me of the way the skies quiet just before a tornado strikes, taking everything down in it's path.

After about an hour I retreat to my bedroom. There is no telling how much longer they will be in there, but I can't stand to just sit on the couch and twiddle my thumbs any more.

The sound of the door knob turning causes me to jump up from the bed, and I all but tackle Alec to the ground once he enters the room.

"Are you okay? What happened? He apologized, right? I told him that-" The word vomit spilling from my lips is halted when he interrupts me.

"Hey, calm down. It went okay, surprisingly. We both had a lot to say to each other, but I guess I'm okay with where we ended things for now." His tone is off, which makes what he is saying seem unconvincing.

I take a step back, "Then why do you sound just as upset now as you were before the talk?"

I can see something swirling behind those green eyes, and I get a queasy feeling in the pit of my stomach.

"Jo, I'm still not staying. I shouldn't have stayed this long. I came home for a reason, but that reason is gone. I should have moved out after my mom died."

Leaving? I try to process his words.

"Okay, so you're moving out. That isn't the worst thing that could happen. I mean, we can make it work." I say, trying to keep a glimmer of positivity through this shit storm we are weathering.

"I've made life hell for my dad. I blamed so much on him, and held so much resentment that I wasn't able to get past my own pain long enough to see that he was hurting too. He fucked up, but so did I." He shoves his hands into his pockets and rocks back and forth on his heels. "This- this thing we have, it isn't good for anyone. I was selfish, so goddamn selfish to do this."

No. Not this shit again.

"Please stop, okay? We already knew that this wouldn't be easy, that it would be hard for people to accept. I thought we'd gotten past that?" I try to keep my voice from shaking, but it's useless.

"What about our parents? You can't look me in the eyes and say it isn't selfish to put whatever this is before their fucking marriage? They're married. That isn't going to change. This... we don't even know what we're doing. You're still so young, and I- well I don't even know if I'm capable of giving you what you need. What you deserve." He reaches for me but I pull away.

"Are you kidding me? Would you stop this self-deprecating bullshit for one second? You can't just push me away because your scared of what could happen. I know you don't actually want to end this, I know your feelings haven't changed after one conversation with your father." I can feel the heat radiating over ever inch of my skin.

"I've been doing a lot of thinking the past few days, and I just don't see how this ends in any way other than me getting the fuck out of here and giving everyone a shot at having some semblance of a normal family. I was so consumed with what I want that I didn't even consider what this would do to my own dad. He's here dealing with this when he should be on his honeymoon. I don't want to be the guy who destroys everything anymore."

The only thing he is destroying right now is my heart. My heart that is now his, totally and completely.

"So what, suddenly you want to be the good guy? You expect me to believe you give a shit about their marriage?" I spit, and he winces.

"I will never be the good guy in this story, but I can remove myself from it. I can go back to school, and try not to be the loser who never makes anything of himself. Jo, you are still in high school. You don't even know what you want out of life yet."

What a cop out. I can't even cry, the rage burning within me is all consuming.

"Stop talking to me like I'm a child, Alec. This is bullshit and you know it. I know what I want, and it's to be with you. I know you want to be with me, too. I know you do. So please, just stop this. I can't take it."

He takes a step towards me again, but this time my feet feel cemented to the floor.

"I don't regret anything, I need you to understand that. You helped me in more ways than I will ever be able to put into words. You showed me I wasn't some fuck up, you made me want to be better. I want to be better, that's why I have to do this. Can't you see that?" His eyes are pleading for me to relent, to accept his pathetic attempt to fall on the sword.

"The only thing you are accomplishing by doing this is shattering my heart. So no, I don't fucking accept it." I say through clenched teeth. "If you expect me to just calmly allow you to walk out of my life then you don't know me at all. Was this all a game to you? That's the only way I can rationalize what you are saying to me. There is no way you could care for me and leave me after everything. Do I mean that little to you?"

My words wound him, I can see the pain that flashes across his face. "You know that isn't true. I'm trying to do the right thing. You're my fucking step sister. I can't be in love with my step sister. Do you understand what people will say? How hard it will be for your mom? My dad? Allie?"

I lose my breath.

"You're in love with me." I say, but it comes out as almost a whisper.

"It doesn't matter, what matters is that I'm putting an end to this while I still can. Just- just don't make this any harder than it already is. I wanted this conversation to go so differently, I thought you would understand."

No, he hoped it would make this easy for him. He hoped that I would make it easier to walk away.

"Get the fuck out." I say. "I won't listen to another word."

"Jo, please. Don't-"

"Get out." This time it's a scream. A scream that is undoubtedly heard by everyone in the house. "If you want to leave me then do it. Don't be a coward and just do it." I shove my hands into his chest. "Go. Leave. You were always going to hurt me, we both knew that. It was inevitable. Don't you dare blame this on doing the right thing, though. You're scared. You are terrified because you love me, because it means all you're battle armor has been stripped away and now it's just you. The real you, and you can't fucking handle it."

He says nothing, but that speaks louder than any words ever could.

"Getting caught just gave you the perfect get out of jail free card. You get to run away instead of facing that this is real now. The secrets aren't secrets anymore, and there is nowhere else to hide. That's exactly what you are, Alec Miller. A coward. Now get the fuck out."

Once he leaves and closes the door behind him I fall to my knees. The tears fall freely now, and the rage that fueled me only seconds ago is replaced with a pain that I can feel deep in my bones.

CHAPTER TWENTY-EIGHT

Six months later...
 The alarm on my phone pulls me out of a deep sleep, and for once I am thankful. It's been a while since I had the dream, the one where he shows up and tells me he made a horrible mistake and begs me to forgive him. I always do, and we always have the steamiest makeup sex imaginable. This sounds like the perfect dream, except each time it comes I wake up feeling more empty than the last.

We're headed into spring now, and it's time to start thinking about my future. At least, that's what my school guidance counselor says each time I fail to meet a deadline for a scholarship application. Thanks to Sean's wealth it is no longer required for me to have financial aid to attend college, but it doesn't deter Mrs. Greene from relentlessly hassling me about it.

"You have so much potential, Josephine. I can't stand to see you squander such opportunities away to be ordinary."

I've decided on a few places to apply, but each time I sit down to finish the applications I lose all motivation and end up taking a nap. I have the grades to get in to pretty much any state school, and with the added freedom that comes from having no pesky financial problems to hold me back the options are endless. The problem is that the spark that once burned so fiercely within me was snuffed out. I never wanted to be the girl who got her heart broken and shut down, but fuck it's hard pick up the pieces.

Mom wants me to stay local and go to one of the large universities nearby. That isn't in the cards though, that much I have decided on. I want to get away and start fresh. I want to be somewhere where the memories of what I had with him can't haunt me. At least if I am across the county the only way he can get to me is in my dreams.

"Have you thought about the University of Florida any more? Your mother tells me that was always your plan." Sean asks, trying to start up a bout of normal conversation over breakfast.

"A little." I respond. "I'm not sure about Florida anymore."

"Where are your friends applying?" My mother asks.

A few aren't going to college, instead decided to take up a trade and begin working for an honest wage. My best friend, V, is taking a year off with her boyfriend to travel. My childhood best friend is actually sticking close to his roots and applying to UF, like we always planned. His girlfriend, and my stepsister, are constantly planning out just how incredible their summer is going to be. Especially the trip to Disney that I begrudgingly declined to join them on.

"They're all going to be a bit spread out after we graduate." I say.

My mother's lips form a tight smile, "So when do we get to find out your final choices?"

I've been avoiding this topic, purely out of my own selfishness. I am not ready to see the sadness in her eyes when I reveal that my plan is to move away.

"Applications are due for the most part in the next few days, I'll start getting the responses before too long. I promise as soon as I make a decision you'll be the first to know." I muster the best smile I can manage, and this seems to placate her for the time being.

Three months after that...

I've heard back from all my safety schools at this point, and unsurprisingly I was accepted into all of them. The University of Florida was first, then the University of Alabama came next. The last of my safety schools to come in was the University of South Alabama, which is the closest to home. My mother seemed particularly fond of that option, however I have already ruled it out.

As I sit in front of my laptop constantly hitting the refresh button to check for an update to my application status, I can all but picture my future at UC Berkeley. Their Political Science program is amazing, and the idea of living on the west coast becomes more and more appealing with each passing day. I would still be near the water, so I know my soul would be happy.

A new update has been to your application.

The words finally appear in tiny red lettering next to the 'Check Status' icon, and my heart begins to lurch in my chest.

Here goes nothing.

The screen goes white before the university's seal appears. Streamers of multi-colored confetti begin to fall over the black letters, and the anthem plays in the background. One word changes everything, 'Congratulations.'

A squeal escapes my lips and it doesn't take long before Allie bursts in the room sporting a look of utter confusion. "What the-"

Her eyes locate the celebration happening on my computer screen and she immediately joins me in jumping around the room like a toddler who'd eaten one too many sweets.

"I knew you'd get in!" She says, excitedly. "Holy crap, California? Can you believe this?"

No, I can't to be honest. Up until this moment it had all been hopes and dreams, but now it was real. I was really moving to California. I was actually doing this.

"Mom!" I yell down the stairs. "I got in! I got in to UC Berkeley!"

Sean and my mother cheer from the living room. "Oh honey, that's incredible. I know you are just over the moon!" I hear my mother say. I know without even seeing her that her eyes will be glassy, but a smile on her face nonetheless.

She wasn't exactly thrilled when I told her this was the one, that if they accepted me none of the other colleges would even stand a chance. After touring the campus I was sold, and waiting to find out my fate was excruciating. It was all worth it, though. I am officially a college girl come fall, and for the first time in a long time I feel full of nothing but pure bliss.

"We have to celebrate!" Allie exclaims, her arms still wrapped around me. "Everyone is headed to the docks tonight, we have to go!"

I look down, "Oh, I don't know. I kind of want to stay in, we could order a pizza? Or-"

Allie gives me that look of hers, the one that let's me know I'm going to end up at this party whether I like it or not.

"Nope, not happening. Not tonight. This occasion calls for fun to be had, actual fun." She puts both hands on her hips. "No excuses, and no whining. Now get dressed."

I can't help but smile at her persistence. "Fine, whatever."

I haven't gone out much since the summer ended. Of course everyone has continued to embrace me fully, but it wasn't the same after Alec left. Once the group all realized what went down between the two of us there were mixed reactions to say the least.

Nate tried to be supportive, but they would never be able to truly understand just how much the whole experience affected me. V, on the other hand, spewed bouts of venomous expletives geared at the man who left me. What was it she called him, a no-good shit-for-brains spineless jellyfish?

I always appreciated how she essentially became my hype man, always making sure that I remembered that none of what happened was my fault. She loved to tell me that he never deserved me, and that he did me a favor by bailing.

I don't know that I agree with that, but it makes some days a little easier.

After an hour of being dolled up by my insistent step-sister, we are loaded up in the Jeep and headed for the docks.

I am greeted with lots of hugs and congratulations from the group when we arrive, and before long I am a few drinks in and feeling great. When Nate finally arrives he scoops me up into his large arms and swings me around.

"Well, you did it. You got in to your dream school. How does it feel?" He asks once my feet are back on solid ground.

"Unreal. I still can't really believe it." I answer.

We continue to talk about the big move but I can't help but be distracted at the constant ringing of his phone. Each time he silences it, and with each new call I grow more and more curious.

"Someone really wants to talk to you." I say, trying to get a look at the screen.

"Eh, it'll be alright. I can call him back later." He says, sliding the phone back into the pocket of his jeans.

He?

I want to ask, but I know I shouldn't.

The sudden awkwardness that overtakes me must be easily recognizable because he nudges me with an elbow, "Hey, you need another drink."

He turns to walk towards the cooler but I stop him. "Is it him?" I ask, quietly.

He seems to consider his response for a moment, but eventually nods. "He's, um, coming to visit. He's probably calling to make sure it's still a good weekend."

All the breath leaves my lungs.

"Oh." Is all I can manage.

I shouldn't be upset that he didn't let me know he was coming home to visit, but I am. We didn't exactly leave things on the best terms, in fact we haven't spoken since the day I told him to get the fuck out.

"Yeah." Nate shifts uncomfortably. "Just for a few days. He's passing through on his way to Savannah."

"Oh." I say again. Fuck why can't I use my words. Use actual words Josephine. "He's been traveling, then?" I ask, thankful for a strand of coherent syllables.

"Yeah. I guess he's trying to find himself or some shit." Nate shrugs.

"What's in Savannah?" I ask, my initial shock seeming to ease a bit.

"Some festival or something, I think." I can tell he wants to change the subject, so I refrain from asking anymore questions.

The rest of the night is a blur. I drink way too much to try and dull the ache taking over my body. Alec will be here. Will I see him? What would we even say to each other? Would he even want to speak to me?

These questions race through my mind until the alcohol finally does the trick, and I slip into a drunken haze.

CHAPTER TWENTY-NINE

If the pounding in my head is any indication of how my night went, I'd rather not be reminded of it. I drank excessively after learning Alec was coming to visit. My last clear memory is downing several cans of cheap beer in an attempt to drown out my own thoughts. I vaguely remember dancing with some guy, what was his name? I think it was Ben? Hell, I don't know.

The image of his hands running over my body begins to form in my mind and it makes me nauseous.

When my eyes finally adjust to the light filling the room from a nearby window I realize that I'm not in my room.

Where the hell am I?

A poster of a football player hangs on the wall, and clothing litters the floor. I jump up from the strange bed, terrified to see who I am sharing it with.

"Would you stay still? Jesus, Jo. What time is it?" Allie's groggy voice calls out from underneath a pillow.

Oh thank God.

"Where are we?" I whisper to my step-sister.

I look around the room again for any hint as to who's room we have invaded.

"Nate's place. You were trashed. I couldn't take you home like that." She answers, peeking out from the mound of pillows. "You feel okay?"

I rub my temples and groan. "I need water. And food. And Advil."

She laughs, and stretches out from beneath the comforter.

A light knock comes from the door. "I hear voices, guess that means you're alive in there."

Nate.

"Barely." I call back to him. "Please tell me you have pain killers."

I study my reflection in the mirror above his dresser. My hair is a mess, though my makeup seems mostly intact.

"Why did you let me drink so much?" I let out a groan.

"Hey, don't blame me. I tried to get you to slow down, but you were on a mission last night."

Nate enters the room and tosses a bottle of Advil towards me. "Ah, you're a life saver."

"Sure, I imagine you'll need it after last night. You, uh, really had a lot to drink." He says, rubbing the back of his neck.

"Don't even mention alcohol. I am never drinking again." I say, falling back onto the bed.

Allie and Nate exchange a look before bursting into a fit of laughter. "Sure." They say in unison.

A memory of the night before creeps into my mind. "Fuck. We have to go, Allie. Where's my keys?"

She looks confused, "Uh, what's the rush? I thought you were hungry?"

I look to Nate, and his eyes flash with recognition.

"Alec is coming. Here. I can't be here."

She says nothing, she doesn't have to. She rises from the bed and points towards my keys on the bedside table.

Nate flashes an apologetic smile, but I know he understands why I have to leave.

"Thanks for letting us crash here." I say, and fall into his body as his wraps an arm around me.

"Of course, anything for you Jo."

I try not to focus on his words too much. I need to get out of this house before Alec shows up.

I don't even know that he would care that I slept here. It isn't like he's made any attempt to contact me since we last spoke, but I can't deny the small part of me that still doesn't want to upset him.

I slip my shoes back on my feet and grab my keys, making a beeline for the exit.

The bright morning sun beaming down shocks my senses as I step out the front door. As if I didn't already regret the amount of alcohol I'd consumed the night before enough already, the constant ache in my head made sure to remind me.

"Can we please get some food?" Allie whined.

I roll my eyes and nod my head.

I pull out of the driveway at the same moment a black motorcycle turns onto the street. I do not know how I know it's him, but I do. I can feel my heart pounding, and as I lock eyes with the driver, I wish more than anything I could disappear.

"Oh." I hear Allie murmur under her breath.

Time stops for what seems like an eternity. The person who is responsible for both igniting the fire inside me and snuffing it out is staring at me with an intensity that makes my skin buzz with electricity.

"Jo, you okay?" My stepsister asks quietly.

I don't speak, I can't.

Instead, I drive away. I keep my eyes on the road, and try with everything still left inside me not to look back.

"You haven't spoken in an hour, Jo. Just talk to me, I can help." Allie begs.

I know she wants to, but there is no way she can help me. Nothing could have prepared me for the look in Alec's eyes when he saw me leaving Nate's house so early in the morning.

Betrayal. Confusion. Hurt. Anger.

My heart hurts. That is the only way I can describe what I am feeling right now.

I know what he must have thought, and it kills me.

"I don't want to talk about it." I say, plainly.

Allie closes the space between us and plops down onto the sofa next to me. "That's not true, and we both know it."

It is true, though. I have nothing to say. There are no words, only pain. I thought I was getting over what happened between us, but today proved I was just lying to myself. That I was simply in denial about how badly I was broken.

"I'm not dropping this." She says, and I know she means it.

"Allie, you didn't see the way he looked at me. He thought- he thought I stayed with Nate. I can tell." I say, relenting.

She laughs. She actually fucking laughs.

"I fail to see what is funny, Al." I say, not even attempting to hide the frustration in my voice.

She raises an eyebrow, "Seriously? After what he did, you are worried that he thinks you're with Nate? Good! He deserves to sweat. Who the hell cares what he thinks. He left you, Jo. He's the one who skipped town and left you to pick up the pieces." Her arm wraps around me. "I love my brother, but that doesn't mean I feel bad for him in this situation. I hope he does think something happened, and I hope it's eating him alive."

Her blunt response surprises me, but she's right.

He did leave me. He made the decision to remove himself from my life, so why do I care if he is upset? I have done nothing wrong. Alec Miller is not the victim in this story.

My phone buzzes next to me, and when I see a message from Nate come through I know it can't be good.

Nate: He's pissed. I tried to tell him why you were here, but there's no talking to him right now. He left, just giving you a heads up in case he shows up.

"Fuck." I exclaim loudly.

Allie shifts, "My brother?"

I shake my head, "It's Nate. He thinks Alec is coming here, to confront me I guess. Allie, I can't do this."

"Just go to your room, I'll handle it." She says, and for a brief moment I almost want to stay. To hear him out, to see him face to face again. But the moment is brief, and I retreat towards the stairs.

I am thankful that Sean and my mother are out for the day. There is no telling how this would blow up if they were home.

It doesn't take long for the sound of hushed voices downstairs to seep through the walls.

While I can't make out what they are saying at first, the volume continues to rise.

"She doesn't want to see you, Alec. Why can't you wrap your mind around that?" I hear Allie say to her brother. "Just stop!"

"We both know I'm getting up those stairs." He yells back.

"Where have you been? You know we've all been worried. You just disappear for months and expect to show back up and break her heart all over again? No. I won't let you. We were the ones who had to watch her cry, not you. Just leave it alone, I'm serious." Allie's voice is shaky now.

"I did what was best, for her. Okay? Just let me talk to her." He isn't relenting.

The sound of his voice causes a war within me. Part of me wants to throw open the door and go to him, and the other wants to stay locked in this room where he can't hurt me.

The war wages on, and I am not sure which side will win.

Before I have to make the decision, the thud of heavy footsteps against the wooden stairs snaps me back into reality.

I know he's standing outside the door. I can hear his labored breathing.

"Jo?" His voice is pained.

I try to speak, but nothing comes out.

"Look, I know you don't want to see me. You don't have to open the door, just listen. Okay?" The pleading in his words shakes me to my core.

I hold my breath, bracing myself for whatever he is about to say.

CHAPTER THIRTY

I keep my distance from the door, almost as if doing so offers me some sense of safety from this situation. I say nothing.

"I deserve that, the silent treatment. I get it." Alec says in a low, defeated voice. "I just- I just need you to understand. I didn't want to hurt you, but I know that's exactly what I did. I thought you would be pissed for a few days and then realize it was for the best. You know? I mean, why would you want to be with someone like me? I'm nothing. And you, well Jo- you are everything."

My cheeks flash with a surge of heat, and if I could slap him right now I would. How dare he? How dare he make that choice for me.

"You're so young, and you have this entire life ahead of you that is just getting started. You don't want to be the girl who fucked all of that up to screw around with her stepbrother."

I can't hold in my anger any longer. "Screwing around?" I scream. "That's all we were, huh? Fuck you, Alec."

I can tell my outburst has shaken him. He didn't expect for me to speak. "What? No! That isn't what I meant. God, I suck at this. Can you just open the door?"

I shake my head, but obviously he can't see that.

"I didn't mean it like that. You know it was more, it was so much more. That's what everyone else will think, though. This, you and me, it doesn't work in the real world. It only worked when it was a secret. When other's opinions weren't involved. Even then, I don't think either of us really thought about what being together would mean."

The tears are welling in my eyes again, and the wave of nausea crashing into me is too much.

"I know you hate me, and maybe that is for the best. Maybe it will be easier for you to move on if you hate me. But Jo, Nate? Please don't. I know he'd do anything to have you, but I can't handle that. It would kill me. You know that." The desperation in his voice does nothing but anger me more.

I throw open the door and shove my hands into his chest.

"Hate you?" I scream, tears rolling down my face. "I wish I could fucking hate you. Everything would be so much easier if I could."

Alec takes a step back, his face riddled with pain.

"Nate let us stay there because I was wasted. Allie didn't want to bring me home like that. There is nothing happening between us, not that it's any of your damned business. You gave up the right to have a say in what I do when you walked out on me."

I shove him again, hoping that it would somehow make me feel better. It didn't.

"You are a coward, Alec. A fucking coward. You didn't leave because it would be *better for me*. You left because shit got real and you couldn't handle it." I repeat the sentiments from our last conversation, and his face falls. I know hearing them again hurt him.

"The mighty Alec Miller fell in love, and he was too damn scared to do anything about it. You want to pretend you did the right thing? Whatever, go right ahead. Whatever helps you sleep at night."

I take a step back, and fear flashes in his eyes when he realizes I am about to walk away.

"Jo, I-"

I hold up my hand to stop him. "What's the point?" I say, almost in a whisper.

"What?" He asks,

"What's the point of saying anything else? Nothing will change.

I'm moving, you know? To California. I got into UC Berkeley. I wanted to get as far away from this place as possible. Do you know why?"

I don't wait for him to answer. "Because being here, in this house, in this town- it's excruciating. I can't escape you. Even after you're gone, the memories are still here. They are haunting. I may be young, but I fell so hard for you it hurts. I am so in love with you that even after everything you did, I still feel the same way. I guess that makes me the idiot here."

He closes the space between us and places his hand on my cheek. His touch causes an explosion within me.

"You can't be in love with me, Jo. I don't deserve you." He manages to say.

"That's the thing about love, it doesn't seem to give a shit about things like that." I reply, moving away from his reach. "You are right about one thing, though. I will move on. Eventually. But not because it's what I want. It will be because you made that decision for the both of us."

The sound of the front door opening causes us to break the intense eye contact, and within seconds I hear Sean yell his son's name.

"Alec, what the hell are you doing here?" The fury in his eyes as he takes in my tear streaked face is unmistakable.

I know that my mother is downstairs, and I immediately want to run to her. I want to let her hold me, for her to make the pain stop.

"Dad, I just needed to talk to her." Alec's voice remains eerily calm.

"Josephine, are you alright?" Sean's attention snaps to me, and I nod weakly.

I take the opportunity to make my escape down the stairs, much to the horror of Alec.

"No, don't. You can't say that to me and then just-"

I cut him off again, "Run away? Why? You did." And with that I turn my back on him and walk away.

CHAPTER THIRTY-ONE

I fall into my mother's arms when I reach the bottom of the stairs. Allie's eyes are holding back tears as well.

"I'm sorry, I texted my dad. I was just worried, he was so angry. I didn't know what would happen." The tears finally fall from her eyes, and I can't blame her for being afraid.

"Honey, are you alright? Did he hurt you?" My mother asks, and the insinuation that Alec would put his hands on me brings out a surprising surge of anger.

"Of course not, he would never touch me. Not in that way." She seems surprised that I am so defensive.

The yelling coming from the top of the stairs doesn't seem to cease.

"You promised this was done. You promised you would leave her alone, son." Sean booms.

"It isn't that simple, dad. I just need to talk to her, please." Alec pleads.

He sounds so broken.

"Of course it is. Whatever happened is in the past, and we're finished with it. This is ridiculous." I imagine Sean throwing up his hands in exasperation.

Alec bounds down the stairs, and my mother stands protectively in front of me.

"Did you mean that?" He asks me, looking straight past my mother's hard eyes. "Answer me, Jo. Did you mean what you just said?"

I am shaking, and no words seem to form.

"Alec, that's enough. Can't you see the state she's in?" My mother says, more harshly than I've ever heard her speak to anyone.

He ignores her, instead keeping his gaze fixed on mine.

"Did you mean it? That your feelings haven't changed? Even after all this? After what I did?" He asks again, desperation thick in his voice.

This conversation shouldn't be happening in front of everyone. I can feel their eyes on me, waiting for me to answer him. Waiting for me to reject him, and judging how long it is taking me to do so.

His eyes seem hollow, all except for the tiniest glimmer that seems to be holding on to a shred of hope that I will say yes. That I meant every word that I said.

What happens if I do? What will that change?

Only moments ago he gave me no inclination that his thoughts on our relationship had changed. He was still justifying his decision to leave me. The fear that admitting my own feelings would still end with him walking out that door overwhelm me.

Did my admission change something for him? Was he so caught up in all of this that he really didn't see that I was in love with him? How could that be possible. It was so obvious, at least I thought it was.

Now who's the coward.

I gather every ounce of strength left in me and speak, tears still falling from my eyes. "Of course I meant it, you fucking idiot."

My mother's grip on me loosens, and I can tell my words have shocked her. Allie lets out an audible gasp. Alec's eyes light up, and one side of his mouth turns into a boyish grin. That stupid grin that I love so much.

"You need to leave." Sean says, and this time Alec nods.

"Sure, but not without her." He says, and my heart slams into my chest.

Sean laughs, "You've lost your mind."

Apparently we both have.

"She's eighteen, if she wants to leave she can." He looks at me and smiles. "She loves me. I don't know why she loves me, but she does. I don't deserve it, but fuck I love her too. I'll be damned if I walk out of this house again without her. I won't make the same mistake twice."

Silence fills the room following his admission. Time seems to stand still.

My mother's concerned eyes meet my own. "You can't possibly be thinking of going anywhere with him. Look at you, honey. Look what he's done to you."

I consider her words, and look back to Alec and smile through the tears. I feel absolutely insane for smiling, but he just admitted out loud that he loves me. Those three words that I never thought he would ever say, he said.

We're now both grinning, and everyone is looking back and forth between us as if we've both gone off the deep end. To be honest, we have.

"So you'll come with me?" He asks, and I can see the fear that I will say no.

"No, she won't. Alec, enough. This has gone too far." Sean says, moving towards his son.

"Yes I am." I say, surprised by the confidence in my words.

You could cut the tension filling the room with a knife.

"What?" My mother, Sean, and Allie all say at once.

"You heard her." Alec says, holding out his hand for me to take.

I do, and when our fingers lace together I feel that fire within me reignite.

All the pain isn't gone, of course. Everything that happened is still there, and there are still so many things we have to figure out. Right now, in this moment, those things don't seem so impossible anymore. I know it will be hard. I know we will both have to fight hard for this, but the important thing is we both want to fight for it.

"I may regret this one day, in fact there is a good chance I will." I say, "But I will never forgive myself if I don't try."

I turn to face my mother. "I love him. I love him so much, and despite everything that has happened... I still want to be with him. I know you can't understand, hell I don't even understand, but this is what I want."

She says nothing, but she doesn't have to. I don't expect anyone to agree with our decision.

Alec leads me out of the house, and when the door shuts behind us I feel like I can finally breathe.

"Did that really just happen?" I ask him.

He squeezes my hand, "Yeah, I think it did."

We walk to the bike, and I stop and stare at the helmet in his outstretched hand. "Don't leave me again, Alec. I can't take it. If we're doing this, we're really doing it."

He presses his body against me and places his hands against my cheeks. "Life was hell without you, Jo. You were right, I was scared. I'm still fucking terrified. I have no clue how to be what you need in a man, but I promise I'll do whatever it takes to figure it out."

I press my forehead to his chest. "You have no idea how long I've waited to hear you say that."

He tilts my face up so our eyes meet, "I'm sorry for making you wait so long."

"Can you say it again? What you said inside? Please." I ask.

That boyish grin is back, "I love you, Josephine. I have fucked up so many things in my life, but you are the one thing I don't want to ruin."

Our lips crash into each other, and all the pent-up emotion from all these months is released.

"Say it again." I breathe out.

"I" He places a kiss on my forehead. "Love" Then another on my nose. "You." And another on my lips.

"Don't make me regret this." I say.

"I can't promise it will always be perfect. I'm going to piss you off, that will never change. I've never done this before. I'll screw up, but I promise you I'll never walk away again."

I can't ask for more than that, it's everything I have ever wanted to hear from him.

"What about California? I graduate in less than two months." I ask, hating that reality has to break through into this moment.

"It's a good thing I haven't put roots down anywhere since I left, California seems as good a place as any." He replies, placing his hand on my thigh.

"Really? You'd move there for me?"

He laughs, "I thought that was sort of obvious after everything that just happened."

I pinch myself.

"What was that?" He asks, amused.

"Oh, you know, just making sure this isn't a dream." I say with a giggle.

As we drive away from the house a flood of emotion washes over me. I wrap my arms around his waist and lace my fingers together, holding on to the man I love with everything I have. I know when I come back home I will have to face a barrage of questions from my family. I know that there is no guarantee they will ever be supportive of us together, and neither one of us could blame them for that.

I can only hope that they will love us through it, and eventually the rest will fall into place.

EPILOGUE

One Year Later...

O I struggle to balance my books in one hand and dig out my apartment key from my purse with the other.

"Dammit" I curse, as my Constitutional Law textbook tumbles to the ground. I finally fish out the key, and slide it into the lock. The smell of Chinese takeout fills my nostrils, and I can almost taste the General Tso's chicken.

"God, I'm starving." I say, plopping down my books onto the counter.

"Didn't feel like cooking, so takeout it is." Alec replies, placing a kiss on my forehead. "How was class?"

I groan. This class was kicking my ass, but I just have to keep telling myself it will all be worth it in the end. "Same as always, lots of case law to memorize. What about you?"

Alec had enrolled in Berkeley City College, a community college right near my university. He was taking a few classes here and there while working.

"Class is class, nothing too exciting to report."

He wraps me in his arms, and I breathe in his scent.

Oh, how I love this man.

This last year had been anything but easy. Those last two months at home had been hell, and I had to deal with constantly being told by my mother and Sean how big of a mistake I was making. Allie, on the other hand, tried to be a bit more supportive. Even so, she wasn't sold on the idea.

Our relationship had been a roller-coaster to say the least. One of those old wooden rollercoasters that gave you whiplash every time you rode it. It began fast, ended even faster, and then in the blink of an eye we were trying to make things work again. See, whiplash.

The beauty of California was that no one knew anything about us. Here, we are just Jo and Alec. A completely normal couple without the soap opera-esque background.

"You know, I'm hungry too." Alec says, his eyes hooded with mischief.

"Good thing you got Chinese then." I say.

"Hmm... not for food." He slings me over his shoulder in one swift move and races towards our bedroom.

I giggle and playfully slap his back, "Put me down!"

He lays me onto the bed and hovers over me, peppering kisses from my face down to the curve of my neck.

"You look incredible today." He says in a low voice.

"You say that every day." I quip, rolling my eyes.

His hands snake around my waist and pull the shirt over my head.

He continues the trail of kisses down my body and stops at my hip bone. I let out a small moan and I can feel him grin against my skin.

"You're such a tease." I complain, wanting more.

He slowly undoes my jeans and slides them down my legs.

"You are so fucking beautiful." He breathes into me.

When his hard length presses into me I can't help but gasp. I will never get tired of this.

His rhythm is slow at first, taking his time. Worshiping every inch of my body in the process.

"Harder." I beg, and he obliges.

He flips me over and grasps my hips as he rocks into me over and over. I can feel my release building with each thrust, and I know he is close too when his grip on me tightens as he slams home.

We explode around each other, and he collapses into me. His hands trail the curves of my body as we breathe heavily following our climax.

I turn over and wrap my arms around him, nuzzling into the crook of his neck. I place a single kiss there, and feel my entire body relax.

This is what pure bliss feels like. Coming home to the man I love and getting to experience *this*.

Three years later...

"What do you mean? He's perfect!" I say to Alec.

I point to the scruffy looking dog in the last kennel. He has one tooth peeking out from his mouth, and lopsided ears that look seriously out of place.

"It looks deranged." He says flatly, eyebrows raised.

"That's Frank. He's been with us the longest. He's a sweet fellow, but for some reason no one has chosen him yet." The human shelter employee, Shannon, informs us.

"I can see why." Alec mutters under his breath.

I glare at him, and he throws up his hands in defeat. I always win.

"He's the one." I say, and my boyfriend rolls his eyes.

"Fantastic! Frank, do you want to go home with these nice people?" Shannon asks the dog. He replies with a bark.

"See, he loves us already." I beam, and Alec shakes his head in exasperation.

"Whatever you say, babe."

When we arrive back at home, I show our new pup around. "And this is your bed," I point to a fluffy dog bed right next to ours.

"But you can sleep with me if you like." I whisper to him.

"I heard that." Alec says, wrapping his arms around my waist.

I smile up at him.

I pull out my phone and click to FaceTime my mother. She answers almost immediately.

"Josephine! How are you?" She exclaims. "Sean! It's them!"

"We have exciting news!" I say, sporting the world's biggest grin on my face.

"Oh really, what's that?" Sean asks as he settles onto the sofa beside my mother.

"We've decided to add a new member to the family!"

My mother squeals, "Oh! That's fantastic, I'd hoped you'd wait until after graduation. Or, maybe a marriage. -"

"Jesus Christ," Alec yells. "A dog. We adopted a dog!"

He holds up our new furry friend, and I can't help but laugh at the miscommunication.

"Thank God." Sean exhales, and I laugh again.

"His name is Frank, isn't he adorable?" I ask.

"He's something, that's for sure." Sean remarks, and Alex nudges me as if to say I told you so.

I don't care if he looks a little different, he's perfect.

We catch each other up on everything for a few more minutes, and the call ends with a promise to come home soon for a visit.

When we hang up, I plant a kiss on Alec's lips. Frank growls, and he narrows his eyes. "Look here, buddy. She's mine."

I take in the moment, the three of us piled onto our bed and am once again reminded at how wonderful this life is.

Our road to happiness was never easy, but we made it. I graduate in less than a year, and Alec has decided to get his contractor's license. He is already working with a company, but once he completes the licensing, he will start his own thanks to a sizable investment from his father.

Alec still drives me crazy on most days, but there has not been a single moment that I have regretted what we have- or this life that we have built together.

Our story was never meant to be a fairy tale. It was raw and hard, unconventional, and challenging, but beautiful at the same time. It is our story, and that is all that matters.